She hadn't exactly been sold into slavery, but the result was pretty much the same.

At the time, Valarie thought she was making a good deal: She was getting out of a certain jail sentence and getting a job at the same time. Harvey was unpleasant and dirty, but he offered her a home and a steady income to feed her habit. She was the perfect girl for his massage parlour — street wise but innocent — just what his customers wanted. By the time Valarie realized how dangerous her new "home" was, she was trapped. Would she ever be truly free again?

Valarie

John Benton

Fleming H. Revell Company
Old Tappan, New Jersey

ISBN: 0-8007-8430-8
A New Hope Book
Copyright © 1982 by John Benton
All rights reserved
Printed in the United States of America
This is an original New Hope Book, published by
New Hope Books, a division of Fleming H. Revell
Company, Old Tappan, New Jersey

TO my good friend
Sally Alster,
whose enthusiasm, untiring efforts, dedication, and
willingness to help others, is a source of great inspiration
to all of us at the home

Valarie

1

Bone-chilling wind whipped through my nearly threadbare coat as I huddled up against a building. How I hated winter. And what I wouldn't give for a nice, warm coat!

Times Square just had to be the coldest place in the world in the winter. And I had to stand out here every night!

Shivering almost uncontrollably, I drew my thin coat around me. Sensations in my body told me I had to have drugs before long, or I was going to get sick. To get drugs, I had to have money. And to get money, I sold my body. It wasn't something I was proud of; it was the only thing I knew to do. I was hooked, trapped, hopeless. But if I could just get off again, maybe I'd forget. . . .

Pounding my hands against my arms to try to warm myself a little, I hurried to the corner of Forty-second and Eighth to take a quick look around. I realized that most of the perverts hung around here, so I had to be careful. Usually I had better luck up at Forty-fourth and Eighth. But occasionally I'd pick up a real big spender at Forty-second and Eighth. Businessmen who had heard it was easy to pick up a prostitute on Times Square would always come to Forty-second and Eighth the first time. But some of the perverts dressed like businessmen. Some of them were businessmen. So a girl had to be careful.

9

I had decided I didn't want a pimp, so I had to be all the more careful. I was out here strictly on my own.

I stood there shivering for about five minutes at Forty-second and Eighth. There just wasn't anything going on tonight. But I had to get some money.

Then I saw a sharp-looking guy walking toward me. When he was a few feet away, I stepped in front of him, smiled seductively, and asked, "Want to have a good time?"

He stopped, and his eyes looked me up and down. This was a pushover!

"You want to have a good time?" I repeated.

When he smiled, I knew I had him. But to my shock he sidestepped me and moved on. What on earth was the matter? I knew I was better looking than most of the girls on the street.

I stood there, hands on hips, watching him walk away. I just knew it was a perfect setup. So why did he reject me?

I noticed he stopped at the end of the block and stood there. When he turned and looked back, I gave him a little wave. But he quickly looked the other way.

Maybe the poor guy was scared. Maybe he was having a guilt trip because he had a wife and kids back home. Well, his guilt feelings were no problem to me. I could make him forget those for a while. Besides, I really needed the money, so I decided to go after him. He looked like my best bet right now.

I walked up to him and as seductively as I could I said, "Come on, mister, I'll give you a good time. How about it?"

He looked as though he was going to say yes. But suddenly he turned on me and snarled, "Get lost, sister! I don't want any filthy tramp hanging around me!"

This guy was something else! I couldn't get over the way

he changed so suddenly. Maybe I'd better back off. Maybe I'd come on too strong.

I walked halfway up the block and leaned up against a wall where I could watch him. Now he was also leaning up against a wall, watching me. Something sure was unusual about this guy. But what?

A few other men walked by, and I popped my usual question. Nobody responded. What was I going to do?

I decided to head up to Forty-fourth Street. But there an old grump saw me and yelled, "You're going to get it! I mean, you're really going to get it! You dirty scum!"

He was obviously a pervert, and I wanted to get as far away from him as possible, so I kept walking. I always carried a switchblade, and twice I had had to use it on creeps like that old grump. Sometimes these perverts would kill a prostitute and cut her up into little pieces and stuff the pieces into the garbage or flush them down the toilet. They seemed to feel they were doing everybody a favor to kill a prostitute!

When I got to Forty-eighth Street, it didn't seem as cold. Maybe it was because I was puffing a little from walking so fast. But it still seemed to me that Times Square had the coldest canyons in the world—that it was worse than the North Pole. The tall buildings kept the sunshine from the streets in the daytime. And that shade seemed to breed below-zero cold at night. Would summer never come again?

I knew I had to get off before long, or I'd be freezing to death. Going without drugs for a few hours, with my kind of habit, made you feel as though you were inside a refrigerator.

When a guy walked by, I was so desperate that when I stepped in front of him, I said, "Hey, mister, how about it?"

"Young lady, I'm not that kind of person," he said kindly. "But I've got some good news that'll warm your heart!"

"Good news? Warm?" I responded. "You've got to be kidding!"

He smiled broadly as he said, "Haven't you heard that Jesus Christ died on the cross for your sins, and He wants to forgive you and deliver you from this kind of life?"

Just my luck—a religious nut. There seemed to be one or two of them around every night—even when it was this cold. They all talked about how Jesus could save. Well, that was the farthest thing from my mind at the moment. I didn't need saving. What I needed was money to buy drugs.

"Hey, mister, let's cut the chatter and go out. Okay?"

He was still smiling as he said, "Young lady, if you'd only receive Jesus as your Saviour, your life would be so different!"

Seeing I wasn't going to interest him in anything, I spat out the words: "Bug off, creep! I've got work to do!"

The guy started to say something else, so I wheeled and walked away. I heard him yelling something like, "Try Jesus." Ha! Religion wasn't what I needed. I needed a guy so I could get money and get off!

I guess the religious nut realized I wasn't about to be his customer, so he started up the street away from me in search of some other soul that needed saving. Good! At least I was safe!

I had just leaned up against a building to survey the prospects when I spotted Sheila walking toward me. As she got closer, I noticed she looked terribly upset. Had some pervert ripped her off?

"Sheila, what's the matter?" I called. "You look as though you lost your best friend."

She didn't respond but simply kept walking toward me. That's when I noticed the tears streaming down her cheeks.

Sheila had always been a frail one. Her eyes were sunken in her thin face. She looked as though a strong wind would blow her over. She shouldn't be out on a night like this. But we prostitutes and junkies all faced the same problem: we needed money to survive, money for drugs. We were on a never-ending vicious circle.

I'd known Sheila for about two years now and was surprised she had lasted this long in this jungle. She just didn't have the stamina for this kind of life. But who did?

She was right in front of me now, and I sympathized, "Sheila, it can't be all that bad."

She put her hand over her mouth to try to muffle her sobs, so I put my arm around her. Maybe she just couldn't take this frigid weather. "Listen, Sheila, it'll be okay," I told her.

That's when she looked up at me and wailed, "They took my little girl away from me today!"

"Little Becky?"

"Yes, they came and took her. I mean, they knocked down the door to my apartment and snatched her right out of my arms. She was kicking and screaming and—"

"Who in the world are 'they'?" I interrupted.

"The people from the Bureau of Child Welfare. Somebody reported me, said I was abusing her. I wouldn't abuse my little baby. She's a precious little doll to me. She's the only thing I have! Now she's gone!"

Sheila threw herself against me and sobbed uncontrollably. I patted her, trying to comfort her. But I knew the odds against her getting Becky back must be at least a million to one.

Becky was about three, I guess. I'd seen her out on the streets a few times. I knew that no mother who was a junkie could possibly take care of a child. When Becky adjusted, she'd probably be better off in someone else's home as a ward of the court. But I could tell Sheila sure didn't think so!

"Valarie, she was the only thing I had," Sheila told me between sobs. "The only thing. Now I have nothing. Absolutely nothing!"

Trying to help her see that it was probably for the best, I said, "Sheila, just think. Tonight she's in a place where it is nice and warm. She's had a good supper and been put in a nice, clean bed by someone who really cares for her. You want that for her, don't you?"

She pushed away and looked me straight in the eye. "What's the matter with you, Valarie?" she shouted. "Don't you understand? Becky is my daughter! I gave her life. And she's the only thing I have to live for. Now that they've taken her from me, my world has come crashing to an end!"

"Hey, it really hasn't, Sheila!" I said, trying to comfort her. "This kind of thing has happened before. Why don't you sign yourself into a detoxification program and get straightened out? Maybe if you got straightened out, those people would give Becky back to you."

"How I wish!" Sheila responded wistfully. "But I tried that. I went to a detox center two months ago. Within an hour after I came out I had a needle in my arm! I've tried everything, Valarie. There's nothing that can help me—absolutely nothing. And now my precious baby is gone!"

Sheila was so overcome with grief that I knew that no rational argument would help. I'd try another angle.

"Tell you what, Sheila," I said. "I'll pick up a trick and make a few bucks. Then after I buy some dope, I'll give you some. How about that?"

When Sheila shook her head, I knew she really was grieving. No junkie would reject free dope!

"The only way I'll shoot up again," Sheila told me, "is if I take a hot shot. I don't want to live anymore."

"Come on now, Sheila; that's no way to talk. I mean, you've still got something to live for. Becky's not dead, and—"

"Don't be stupid, Valarie!" she interrupted. "I know I'll never get Becky back. I know what the courts will do. They'll declare me an unfit mother. They'll say I didn't take care of her. They'll say I didn't feed her properly, that I didn't get her proper clothes. They'll say I left her alone in the apartment while I went out, and on and on. You know as well as I do that there's no way I'm going to get my precious little darling back!"

Once again she threw her arms around me and sobbed, looking for the comfort that I couldn't possibly give her. What could I do? What she was saying was true. She probably would never see her little Becky again. Her world really had come to an end.

As I held her, I happened to glance around. Standing a few feet away I spotted the same guy who had turned me down on Forty-second Street. Had he tailed me up here? Right now he was studying both of us. His manner so irritated me that I looked away, trying to control myself.

As I turned away, I saw a guy coming toward us. He looked like a live one! Without a second thought I pushed Sheila away from me. I had to get this one!

He was a few feet away now, so I stepped out in front of him, smiled beguilingly, and said, "Hey, mister, want to have a good time?"

Without a moment's hesitation he replied. "Sure. Why not?"

I grabbed his arm because I wasn't about to let this one get away! My stomach had started churning, and my head was spinning. At any moment I'd vomit. So I had to have this one. Then I'd get my drugs and get off.

We walked on down to Forty-sixth Street, to a hotel I used. I paid the clerk five dollars for a room, and clutching the guy, led him to it.

Inside the room I shut the door and said, "Business before pleasure." The guy kept smiling. Now that worried me. Was he a cop?

He reached into his pocket, and I held my breath. Would he bring out some money—or a badge?

I breathed a little easier when he pulled out a wad of bills and asked, "How much?"

When I looked at that wad, I started calculating. Sometimes when I was desperate, I'd ask for twenty bucks. Sometimes forty or fifty. But if I could get more.... "A hundred bucks," I blurted out. Would he go for it?

He jerked back in surprise. "Hey, who are you anyway?" he asked. "The girls in Chicago don't charge that much!"

"You have to understand, mister, that you are with a New York City girl," I purred. "I mean, a *real* New York City girl. I can do a lot more for you!"

I gave him my most winning smile. He had too much money for me to settle for less. That would buy enough dope for me and for poor Sheila.

When he hesitated, I started putting my coat back on. "Look, mister, I've got a lot of customers waiting out there. So give me the hundred or just forget it."

My bluff worked! "Okay," he said reluctantly, peeling off five twenties and handing them to me.

Too bad all tricks weren't this easy. I'd soon be a millionaire—if I didn't spend it all on dope!

When we got back to the street, the guy said, "You New

York City girls *are* special. I'll be back in town in a month, and I'll look you up. Okay?"

"Great, mister. Anytime!"

But I was really wondering if I'd still be around in another month. In this business one never knew. Last week Michelle died—an overdose. The week before that it was Grace—killed by her pimp. Six months ago Nanette came up missing. No one ever found her. We girls suspected her body probably was dumped into the Hudson River.

In a month's time, where would I be? The thought haunted me as I walked back to Forty-second, bought five bags, and headed for my apartment on Forty-fourth Street, just off Eighth Avenue. Sure, it was dirty and filthy—and not very warm. But it was a roof over my head.

When I was at Forty-third Street I remembered my promise to Sheila. Rats! That would mean walking clear up to Forty-eighth again. It was so terribly cold I almost decided to forget it. After all, she said she didn't want any dope. But I realized that she seemed so desperate that she might kill herself. I'd better go up there and give her a bag. Maybe it would get her mind off her problems long enough to deter her from suicide.

Still shivering and shaking, I made my way to Forty-eighth, but I couldn't find Sheila anywhere. Across the street I spotted Corliss.

I waited for what seemed like an eternity for the light to change and headed to where she stood. "Have you seen Sheila around?" I asked.

"Yeah, she was here just a few minutes ago," Corliss answered. "I noticed her because of the guy who stood there the longest time watching her. He finally got up enough nerve to walk over to her. Would you believe she picked him up?"

That pervert—it couldn't be!

"Was the guy about five-foot-eight and had on a dark blue topcoat?" I asked.

"Yeah, I guess so. I couldn't tell for sure what color his coat was, but it was dark. You know him?"

"No, but a guy like that was bugging me all night. I tried to pick him up on Forty-second Street, but he wouldn't respond. Then he followed me up here. He is perverted. I mean, that guy has got to be perverted."

"Valarie, don't say those words around me," Corliss said with a shudder. "I'm scared to death already. Some of the girls heard there was a pervert around tonight."

"I'm a real dummy," I said. "I was with Sheila when I picked up another guy. I should have warned her, but I was too interested in the money."

Just then my stomach retched, and I vomited all over the sidewalk. Corliss jumped back, fuming. "Valarie, don't puke where I'm standing! Can't you see I'm trying to get a trick? Now who do you think will talk to me here?"

"Excuse me," I said. "But I'm sick, man, really sick."

Corliss grabbed me and pushed me against the building. "There was this trick headed my way," she said disgustedly. "And when you puked, he cut across the street. You cost me that trick, Valarie. I ought to slap you silly!"

I knew I had to get away from Corliss. She was a mean one. If the tricks didn't pay her enough, she'd been known to pull her switchblade and stab them. I'd seen a couple of her victims—bleeding, but afraid to report it to the police.

If she started beating on me now, she'd probably find those five bags and rip me off. Deciding retreat now was the better part of valor, I stumbled away toward my apartment. But I couldn't get Sheila out of my mind. Would that pervert cut her body up into little pieces? And what would happen to Becky? Would she grow up without ever knowing who her real mother was? Maybe I should have tried to find that religious nut. Maybe he could have done something for Sheila.

I quickly put that thought out of my mind. I knew there was no hope for the likes of us. We were hooked—and doomed.

When I got to my apartment, I shot up two bags, saving three for later. Then I went back to the street. It wasn't ten minutes before I got another trick—this time only fifty bucks, though. When I went back out, would you believe I picked up another? This was a young kid, about eighteen. He must have been rich, and I hit him up for a hundred dollars.

I went back to my apartment, got off again, and then went back out into the street and waited a little longer. Since there was no one around, I went back in and shot up another bag.

I thought of quitting for the night. It was so cold, and I was so weary. But I knew I'd get sick again tomorrow if I didn't have my dope. If I got another trick tonight, I'd have enough to buy some bags to get me through tomorrow. Maybe I'd even have enough extra to buy me a warmer coat!

As I stood out in the street shivering, I kept worrying about Sheila. She still hadn't come back. I walked over to the hotel where she and I took our tricks. But Benny, the clerk at the desk, said he hadn't seen her all day. Now I really was scared! I went back out into the street to look for her. I asked around, but no one had seen Sheila. She probably got her wish. That pervert had killed her! Why hadn't I warned her?

I peered into an alley. Had he dumped her body there? I would have walked down to look, but there was no telling what might be waiting there!

Realizing my search was futile and I probably would never see Sheila again, I headed back to the corner. One more trick, and I'd call it a night.

Then I spotted a guy I'd seen before. Whenever I tried to approach him, he always seemed to walk to the other side of the street. But now he was coming right toward me.

It looked like an easy setup. "Want to have a good time?" I asked him, smiling.

If he went for it, this would be number four. And he looked as though he had a lot of money.

He looked me over and then responded, "Sure, why not?"

I took him back to the hotel, got the room, and I shut the door. Again smiling beguilingly, I said, "Business before pleasure."

Without a moment's hesitation he reached into his pocket saying, "Of course! Of course!"

This guy had been around!

I stepped up close, waiting to see what kind of a wad he'd pull out before I told him how much. But he was smart. He asked the price before I saw his money.

"A hundred bucks," I told him, deciding I could negotiate if I had to.

"No problem," he said. He pulled out a huge wad of bills, peeled off two fifties, and handed them to me. As I tucked the money into my purse, I looked up. I couldn't believe it! I was staring at a bright, shiny badge!

"Ma'am, you're under arrest," he was saying. "Let me read you your rights."

I'd heard all this before. In fact, I'd been busted ten times for prostitution. But I never got used to the idea. Being in jail was one of the worst things I had experienced.

He finished reading and slapped handcuffs on me. Then

it hit me that I was going to have to kick my habit in jail—
cold turkey. That would be horrible!

The detective didn't say a word as he took me to the
police precinct. I guess he felt as though he was just doing his job. Well, I sure didn't feel like making conversation!

At the front desk they booked me. The detective asked
my name.

"Susie Smith," I replied.

"Come on; let's not start that nonsense," he chided.
"You're not Susie Smith. I remember a few weeks ago
when Detective Snell nailed you. Your first name's Violet,
isn't it?"

What was the use of lying? With my record they would
soon know my name anyway. So I said, "Have it your way.
The name's Valarie Lambert."

After he filled out a bunch of forms, I was finger-
printed—again. Then they took mug shots—again. I knew
the process by heart by now. But it really made me feel like
a criminal.

From there I was taken down to the first floor, to a sec-
tion where they had six cells for women. They shoved me
into one, and the door clanged shut. The sound ricocheted
down the hallway and made me crumble inside. I'd gotten
off pretty easy every time so far. But this time would they
hit me with a long sentence—maybe as a habitual criminal?
I knew that if I got a mean judge who had gotten up on the
wrong side of the bed, he might put me away for a long
time—especially with my record. And prison was one of
the most horrible places in the world. You had no rights.
You had the lesbians always clawing at you. And you had
to stay put where they told you. There was no freedom to
come and go.

They said I was going to be arraigned in the morning and probably taken out to the prison at Rikers Island if I couldn't make bail.

Dejected at this turn of events, I slumped down on the hard bench. About an hour later I heard someone coming down the hall. Some other poor gal, I supposed, trapped by an undercover cop.

But as she got closer, I recognized her! Sheila! And she looked horrible—all beat up, blood still oozing from the side of her mouth.

Had she resisted arrest? Had that pervert hurt her? What had happened to poor Sheila?

2

Sheila was limping. Some of her clothing was torn. She looked so pitiful, so absolutely forlorn. What in the world had happened to her? How did she get busted?

The matron opened the cell next to mine and shoved Sheila in, with no apparent concern for her injuries. Oh, that matron disgusted me. She was big, fat, sloppy, and arrogant. She probably imagined herself as tough. Well, one of these days she would shove somebody once too often, and she'd get hers!

When I yelled at her about taking it easy with someone who was hurt, she shot back a "mind your own business" at me and then was gone.

I went to the bars separating our cells and said, "What happened, Sheila? You look terrible."

Her sunken eyes reflected her pain and hopelessness. She looked even more sick and frail now. She looked as though she didn't have enough strength to wipe the blood off her face.

When she didn't respond, I asked again, "What happened, Sheila?"

She flopped onto the wooden bench with what looked like her last ounce of energy. Then she dropped her head into her hands and just sat there sobbing.

23

I put my hand through the bars, but I couldn't reach her. "Sheila, for crying out loud, can't you tell me what happened? I'm your friend!"

Her sobs echoed throughout the cell block. Somehow I felt responsible for her condition. I knew I should have warned her about that pervert. She had gone with him. Had he beaten her like this? But how did she get busted, too?

"Sheila, I'm your friend," I said again. "You can tell me."

She finally raised her head, looked at me, and moaned, "My world has come to an end. I don't have Becky anymore. I have no friends, nobody. I'm going to kill myself."

"Hey, I'm your friend," I corrected. "And I know all about Becky. You told me that earlier. I want to know what else happened. Did that pervert beat you up?"

She nodded. "You know when you went off with that guy?" she asked. "Well, this other guy came up to me all smiles. I was getting sick, so without thinking I propositioned him. He told me he wanted to take me to his place. That scared me, but I was desperate for a fix, so I said okay."

I already knew how this was going to end. This kind of thing had happened before—too frequently. He'd taken her down to the deserted docks.

"You know where he took me?" Sheila went on. "He took me down to the docks. I should have known better. But, Valarie, I've used the docks a few times, and it's worked. But not this time!"

I'd used the docks on occasion too. But you really had to be careful. Sometimes the trick beat you up. A pervert would throw you into the water. They found a couple of girls floating down there a couple of weeks earlier. The cops don't worry much about investigating. When they find dead prostitutes and junkies, they figure there's not much sense in checking it out.

"He dragged me into one of those old vacant warehouses," Sheila went on. "Then he started beating on me. Valarie, he was a maniac! If that wasn't bad enough, he pulled out a knife and started slashing at my clothes. I just knew he was planning to cut me up into little pieces. Well, I gave him a good kick you know where. When he doubled over and grabbed himself, I took off. My clothes were half off me, and I had this slash on my face." She pointed.

Oh, how I wanted to slip through those bars and go to her and comfort her, the poor girl!

"When I got back up the street, I started vomiting," she said. "I was desperate for a trick so I could get a fix. I must have been wandering the streets like an idiot. This guy was standing there, and I went up and propositioned him. Much to my surprise, he agreed. Here I was dirty and filthy and bleeding, and my clothes were all in shreds, and this guy agreed to it. I figured he might be another pervert, so I told myself to be careful this time. Well, when we got to the room, he pulled out his badge and arrested me!"

Her head dropped back into her hands, and she started sobbing again. Trying to think of something to comfort her, I said, "Sheila, it's not all that bad. I think that's just a surface cut. You'll be fine. And when we get out, we can spend some time together. You and I can sort of watch out for each other. Okay?"

When she finally raised her head again, I noticed her eyes seemed glassy. She was probably in shock. And even if those were superficial knife wounds, the poor girl needed some medical attention. So I yelled, "Guard! Guard! Come here a minute, will you?"

No response.

I yelled louder, "Somebody help us! Somebody please help us!"

I listened, but all I could hear were Sheila's sobs.

I rattled my cell door, hoping that would attract attention. Maybe they'd at least come and tell me to shut up. But still no sign of anybody.

Once again I yelled as loudly as I could, "Help! Somebody help! Please help!"

Either there was no one out there, or they simply weren't about to respond to the cries of a prisoner.

Sheila was standing up now, looking at the bars. Her actions seemed so deliberate, so determined. It frightened me. And when she started unbuttoning her blouse, I figured she must be in shock.

"Don't take off your blouse," I yelled. "It's too cold."

She acted as though she didn't even hear me. Her attention seemed riveted on something on the ceiling.

She slipped off her blouse and let it drop to the floor.

"Put that back on!" I ordered. "You're really going to be sick if you leave off that blouse!"

Totally ignoring my outburst, she unzipped her jeans and stepped out of them. The girl was out of her head! It was too chilly here in these cells to take off your clothes.

"Sheila, please stop!" I cried. "You're going to catch pneumonia and die!"

She was standing there in her pants and bra, studying the ceiling. I had to get that stupid matron.

Once again I rattled the cell door as hard as I could. I yelled and screamed as loud as I could. But not a sound came from down that hallway.

If I couldn't get the matron, maybe I could detract Sheila and bring her back to reality. Reaching my arm through the cell, I pleaded, "Come over here, please. I want to talk to you."

I figured that if she came over, maybe I could put my arms around her and keep her from freezing. Her jeans and blouse lay crumpled on the floor just beyond my reach.

She acted as if I didn't even exist. Then she took up her clothes, and I breathed a little easier. Maybe she was realizing how cold it was in here. But my relief was short-lived. She was tying a sleeve of her blouse to the leg of her jeans, all the time looking up at the ceiling. My eyes involuntarily followed hers to the top of the cell door. Oh, no! She wasn't thinking about trying to hang herself, was she? That was sure what it looked like!

When she picked up the pant leg that wasn't tied to the blouse and put it around her neck, I let out a blood-curdling scream. If anything would bring help, that should do it!

But no matron responded. I sensed that Sheila's life was in my hands. I was the only one who could help her!

"Sheila! Sheila! I screamed in horror. "Don't do it! Don't do it! Don't! Don't!"

She finally looked in my direction, but her eyes stared vacantly. She was out of her mind! What could I do? I couldn't reason with her. I couldn't get to where she was. I couldn't arouse the matron or the guards. Suddenly I was overwhelmed with a feeling of total helplessness!

She methodically knotted the leg of the jeans around her neck. I pushed my body against the bars that separated us, straining to reach her somehow. But she was about two feet beyond my reach.

"Sheila, look at me!" I whispered. "I love you, honey. I really love you."

She looked at me again—but still with that vacant, blank look. Then she shook her head.

I had to get through to her somehow, so I called, "Sheila, come over here. I've got something sweet and nice to tell you, but I don't want anyone else to hear. Come over and let me hold you in my arms. I love you."

She kept shaking her head, mumbling "Good-bye, Valarie. Good-bye."

"Please, Sheila, please!" I begged. "Not good-bye. Just come over here and let's talk. Come on. Please."

Still shaking her head she said, "Valarie, I know what I'm doing. I'm not crazy. It's just that I have nothing to live for now. My dear little baby is gone. I've been abused by a pervert. I'm full of pain. I'm ashamed of how I'm living. I'm a junkie, and every inch of my body is crying out for dope. I have to prostitute to support my habit. Don't talk to me about love. No one loves me. No one cares about me. In a few minutes it'll be all over."

"Please, Sheila, don't talk that way. I love you. And there's got to be a way out. Don't do it! I'm telling you, don't do it!"

"I have to do it, Valarie. I have to. Inside I'm empty— like a vacuum. I'm shattered. I have nothing to live for now. I can't take all this pain and emptiness. It's the only way out."

She was so determined. What could I do to deter her? And then I thought of the one thing she really cared about.

"What about little Becky?" I asked. "Somebody's going to have to tell that doll that her mommy killed herself. What's that going to do to her?"

"It's got to be this way, Valarie. I can't be a mother to her. I know that. I'm a junkie, and junkies have no hope. The only thing I know how to do is go out on the streets and sell my body. The perverts try to kill me. The cops bust me. I'll do time and go through the agony of kicking here in jail. Then I'll be out on the street again, putting a needle in my arm. I'm trapped! Trapped! Trapped!"

Sheila was screaming now. Maybe her cries would arouse the matron. So I added my shouts to Sheila's screams: "Matron! Matron! Emergency! Come quick! Emergency! Sheila is trying to kill herself!"

I rattled the bars again. Sheila was quiet now, once again studying the bars at the top of the cell door.

I ran again to the bars that separated us and stuck both arms through toward her. "Sheila, if you're going to do it," I said, "at least come over here and hug me good-bye!"

Would she fall for my ruse? If she got close, I would grab those pants away from her. That would end any suicide try.

I waited for what seemed like forever. She took an uncertain step toward me. Then she stopped and said, "Valarie, you can't help me. You're a junkie, too. You live the same kind of life I live. Someday soon you're going to come to the end of your road, too. Some pervert will get you. Maybe he'll kill you. Maybe he'll just torture you so bad that you'll kill yourself to get out of the pain. There's no hope for me. There's no hope for you. Why don't you join me? We can go out together!"

Sheila was right about there not being any hope for us. But I just couldn't bring myself to commit suicide. At least not yet. But maybe if she thought I was. . . .

"Okay, I'll go first," I said. "Give me your jeans."

She took another step toward me, and I reached out. I could almost touch them. If she just came another step nearer, I'd reach her. Suddenly she must have become aware of my intentions, for she jumped back and said, "Use your own pants."

Now I was trapped. "I'll level with you, Sheila," I said. "I don't want to take my own life. I still think there's a glimmer of hope."

"There's no hope, Valarie. You know what happens to girls like us. They die of overdoses. Pimps kill them. They're thrown into the river by perverts. They're cut apart. You know it'll happen to you someday."

"Naw, I'm going to beat this rap, Sheila. You can beat it, too. But please don't do anything to hurt yourself. It just isn't worth it."

I was saying the right words, but down deep inside I knew she was right. There was no hope for the likes of us. But I was going to prolong my life—if I could stand it.

"Good-bye, Valarie," she said softly. "You're the only one who cares what happens to me. But it's good-bye forever."

She walked away from me, flipped the sleeve of her blouse over the bar at the top of the door, reached up, and tied it. Was there nothing I could do to stop her?

In desperation and terror I screamed as loudly as I could: "Somebody help! Somebody help! Sheila is trying to kill herself! Come quick! Come quick!"

I shook the bars with an almost superhuman strength, and the sound ricocheted around the walls. But no one responded.

I suppose the matron was hardened to noises and screams. After all, a lot of prostitutes were also junkies. And girls scream a lot, especially when they're in the agony of kicking.

Sheila had finished tying the knot around the bar. "Don't do it, Sheila!" I screamed over and over and over.

She looked at me and smiled a weak smile. "Good-bye, Valarie. I love you. Tell my baby I really loved her."

With those words she threw her feet out from under herself. I watched, petrified, as the knot tightened around her neck.

"Sheila! Sheila! Don't! Don't do it!" I screamed.

I rattled the bars like a maniac. If that matron would come now, there was still time.

I didn't want to look at her, but I couldn't help myself, I saw her mouth drop open and her tongue come out. She made a gurgling sound, and her body began to shake.

"Sheila, pick yourself up!" I screamed. "There's still time! Pick yourself up! Grab the jeans!"

And she did! She grabbed the leg of the jeans and started to pull herself up! But the poor kid didn't have enough strength, and suddenly she shuddered, and her body fell limp, her hands dropping to her side.

"Sheila! Sheila! Sheila!" I screamed.

Her eyes and mouth were open! She had succeeded. She was dead!

Angry, frustrated, hurting, I screamed, "You murderers! Murderers! Murderers!" I rattled the bars with a new fury. Why couldn't they have responded to my pleas for help? Why did they have to let a poor eighteen-year-old die like that? It was heartless, beastly. And I'd make them pay!

Think of it! I'd had to watch my friend die, and there wasn't one thing I could do to stop her!

In a rage I flung myself down on the hard bench in my cell. Everything broke loose inside of me, and the tears came in torrents. How could that matron be so heartless as not to respond? Didn't anyone care about the likes of us?

When I got to the end, would I do what Sheila did? I looked at my blouse and jeans. Maybe she was right. Maybe it was the only way to go. I was a junkie, too, and a prostitute. The only ones who cared about me were those animal-like creatures who wanted my body for their own use. Maybe I would be better off dead.

I don't know how long I lay there sobbing. But when I

finally heard a door clang at the end of the hallway, I
leaped up and yelled, "Come quick! Sheila has killed herself!"

The footsteps quickened, and there was that sloppy matron with another girl.

"What's all the racket?" the matron demanded.

I pointed toward Sheila's cell—I couldn't bear to look.
"That girl just killed herself. I yelled for you, and—"

The matron gasped when the truth sank in. "Who did
this?" she demanded.

It was such a stupid question that I didn't even try to
reply. "You stay here," she told the girl she was bringing in.
"I'll be right back."

She took off running and soon returned with two male
officers who opened the cell. I watched as one of them un-
tied the knot and Sheila's lifeless body slumped to the
floor. All over again it hit me that this was such a senseless
tragedy. But when I came to the end of my road, as Sheila
had put it, would I do the same?

The two officers carried her body down the hall and
through the door. That was the last time I saw her.

The matron locked the other girl up in another cell,
leaving empty the one Sheila had been in. I don't know
what I would have done if she had been so unfeeling as to
put that girl in Sheila's cell.

About ten minutes later the two officers came back, unlocked my cell, and ordered me to come with them. "We
need to talk to you a few minutes," one of them said.

They led me to a little office and told me to sit down. One
of them sat behind a desk, the other next to me.

"What happened in that cell next to yours?" the one behind the desk asked.

"The girl committed suicide."

"Why didn't you stop her?"

Hey, wait a minute! They weren't going to try to pin the rap on me, were they?

"What do you mean?" I screamed at them. "I yelled. I stomped. I rattled the bars. I did everything I knew how to do to try to get that stupid matron's attention. I tried to talk the girl out of it. She was a friend of mine. I begged. I pleaded, and I cried."

"Why didn't you call for help?" the other cop said, apparently not even listening to what I had just told him. "We were just outside the office there. We could have come down and stopped her. Don't you know that the officials and the public put tremendous pressure on us when somebody commits suicide in jail?"

"Don't give me that nonsense!" I sneered. "I don't care what happens to you. All I know is that I lost a friend tonight—probably because you birds were off playing cards somewhere and couldn't be disturbed. I did everything to try to get someone to come, but nobody came!"

"Now hold on!" the one behind the desk yelled back at me. "Don't you go judging us. For all we know, you're the one who put her up to it. Maybe she had something on you and was going to rat on you in court. You said you knew her. This kind of a deal happens all the time. So tell us what really happened. Maybe we can work it so you get off easy."

I couldn't believe it. They really were going to try to pin the thing on me so they could save their own necks!

"Hey, there's no way you're going to implicate me!" I said. "That girl was a junkie, a prostitute. They took her little girl away today, and she was so despondent. She was almost murdered by a pervert down on the docks. You guys have been around. You know what goes on in the streets. She came to the end. She figured the only way out was to kill herself. I did everything I could to stop her, but I couldn't reach her. And you guys wouldn't respond to my pleas for help."

"Okay, Valarie Lambert, don't go lecturing us. We know what happened. But we want to know why she did it in our jail. Let's get something straight. There's going to be an investigation. People are going to ask questions. So I want to tell you something right now. That girl didn't kill herself because of the conditions in the jail. Do you understand that?"

"Ha!" I sneered. "It was this jail that did her in. It was the last straw. She was cold. She was kicking. And you guys could have saved her life if you had answered my calls for help. So don't try to tell me that the conditions in this jail had nothing to do with it."

The cop sitting next to me jumped up, jerked me from my chair, and shouted, "Listen, sister, I want to tell you something right now. You've got a long record. You're a prostitute and a junkie. No matter what you say, nobody is going to believe you!"

I grabbed his hands and yelled, "Get your filthy hands off of me this minute! I can't wait to get into court. I want to tell the judge the whole story about this stinking jail! I mean, I am going to sing. And both of you guys are going to be in deep trouble. And so is that filthy, sloppy matron! You're all so hardened and unfeeling that you won't even respond to a cry for help!"

The other cop, realizing his buddy had blown it, said, "Calm down, young lady. I know this has been upsetting, and—"

"You'd better believe I'm upset!" I shouted. "And I'm going to tell you something else. I'm not going back to that cell. You send me back there, and I'll hang myself, just like my dear, sweet friend did. And the papers will tell the story about two hangings. And you guys are going to be held responsible!"

"You really are upset, aren't you?" the cop said again.

"I'm furious!" I yelled. "That was a senseless hanging. If you guys or that matron had been on the job, poor Sheila would be alive today. She could go back to her little daughter. But now her daughter's an orphan, and it's your fault!"

I realized I'd gone too far when the cop standing by me slapped me across the face and yelled, "I can't stand a smart-mouthed junkie! Now you know we had nothing to do with that death, don't you?"

I felt my lip swelling and saw him still standing over me, ready to hit me again. So I said, "Okay, okay, I understand."

"Let me tell you something else," the cop behind the desk said. "It's about time you took some responsibility for your own life. Nobody is forcing a needle into your arm. Nobody is forcing you to stand out there on those icy streets to hustle. Why don't you just pull yourself together and straighten up and go home and behave yourself like a good girl?"

I gritted my teeth to keep from shouting at him again. Didn't he know I was hooked? Didn't he know I had to prostitute to support my habit? It would be nice to go home. I'd like to be in a nice, warm bed with clean sheets—instead of screaming at this cop in this horrible jail. But I had no choice. I had no control over the events of my life. I'd made heroin my god, and there was no way out.

"Young lady, if you don't cooperate with us, we can make it pretty tough on you," the cop said. "The records say you were busted for prostitution. Now we can just happen to find a couple of bags of dope in your coat pocket and add possession to that charge. You know what I'm talking about?"

I knew. Sometimes they planted dope on a person so they could make an arrest. And I knew if they did that, I'd be in the slammer for a long, long time.

"Okay, what happens if I cooperate?" I asked. "Suppose I just tell them only the part about how despondent she was over their taking her little girl away, and about being a prostitute and a junkie, and about the pervert. Suppose that's all I tell them. Then what happens?"

Both cops smiled and seemed to relax. "It'll go a lot easier for you," one of them said. "A lot easier."

They were backpaddling now. "We don't want to seem mean or tough or anything like that," the one who slapped me said. "We just want you to tell the truth. We've been getting a lot of flak about suicides in jail. The police commissioner is pulling his hair out and is ready to do some mass firings. Now me and Thomas here, we each have a wife and kids. We can't afford to lose our jobs. Besides, I've got only three more years to retirement. You understand what I'm trying to tell you?"

"What's it worth to you if I keep my mouth shut?" I asked.

"Plenty, baby, plenty!" they echoed in unison.

They put me in a different cell, away from where Sheila had killed herself, locked the door, and went away. I knew I had something on them, and I figured they'd be pretty careful about what they did to me.

Next morning the matron came and unlocked my cell. "Come with me," she said. "I think you're going to be surprised at what happens to you now."

I followed her through several doors until we finally

stood at the front desk. The two officers who had questioned me last night were sitting there, smiling. I was scared to death. They were obviously up to something. What were they planning to do to me to be sure I didn't tell all I knew about last night?

3

Across the room I noticed a short, fat man standing, apparently waiting. Oh, he was ugly! A big cigar protruded from his mouth. I couldn't tell if he was smoking it or chewing it. His soiled brown coat covered similarly dirty blue pants. Neither looked as though they'd ever been cleaned. The stubble of his beard had seen several sunrises.

When I looked back at the two cops and the way they were grinning, I knew something was up.

"Okay, what's so funny?" I demanded.

"Your uncle's come for you," one of them said, nodding in the direction of that fat, ugly bum. "Meet your Uncle Harvey."

"What Uncle Harvey?" I demanded. I had no uncle by that name. In fact, I wouldn't claim that guy as a relative if they paid me. He looked as though he'd just come off of Skid Row.

"This is Harvey Epstone, owner of the Blue Lagoon Massage Parlor," one cop said.

I looked at him and wondered who would want a massage from a filthy thing like Harvey. Just the idea of having his dirty hands on me made chills run down my spine. I was used to all kinds of men, but I wanted nothing to do with one like this!

Harvey walked over to me, extended his grubby hand,

and said, pleasantly enough, "Hi, Valarie. I understand you had the misfortune to get busted."

How did he know about me?

"How do you like it back there in those cells?" he asked.

"You just keep your fat lip shut, mister!" I spouted off. "It's none of your business what I've done or what I like."

"Hey, Valarie, just cool it, will you?" one of the cops said. "This is your Uncle Harvey. You just do what he says, and everything will be okay."

"What do you mean, okay? You know very well everything is not going to be okay. With my record I'm going to do time."

"Oh, but it doesn't have to be that way," the cop responded. "Your good old Uncle Harvey has come to save you!"

They both laughed, and when I looked at Harvey, I saw he was laughing too. "What's the deal?" I demanded.

"I need a young chick like you to help me in my massage parlor," Harvey said. Noticing my raised eyebrows, he hurried to say, "Now don't get me wrong. This business is strictly legit. I mean, all you have to do is give body rubs."

"You've got the wrong chick," I said. "I'm not into that kind of thing."

"What's it worth to you?" he asked.

"What did you say?"

"I said, what's it worth to you?"

"Get me out of jail," I blurted out.

"Done!" he said.

Both of the cops were grinning from ear to ear.

"What in the world is going on?" I asked again.

"Uncle Harvey has already bailed you out of jail," one of them told me, "on condition that you go to work for him. We can let you go if you want—because you'll be gainfully

employed. After our little chat last night, we called Uncle
Harvey and explained your case to him. He agreed to help
you out by offering you a job in his business."

It was beginning to make sense, but I wasn't sure I
wanted to work for this creep. When I hesitated, the cop
said, "Look, Valarie, it's a very simple choice. You can go
to work for Uncle Harvey in his massage parlor, or you can
go to jail. Now which is it going to be?"

I'd never heard of bailing someone out of jail so she
could work in a massage parlor. Well, I was really suspicious of that Harvey. He looked so horrible.

"Suppose I tell Uncle Harvey to take his money and his
business and stuff it up his nose," I said.

"Sure, why don't you be real bright and do that?" one of
the cops said sarcastically. "Then we are going to march
you right back to your cell. And when your case comes before the judge in several months, we're going to tell him
about that bag of heroin we found in your coat pocket!
Don't be a fool, Valarie. He's already posted bail. You can
walk right out that door now if you go to work for Harvey."

"What kind of business is it?"

"A massage parlor, dummy. Don't you know what a
massage parlor is?"

I had to admit I'd seen plenty of them around. I'd
watched guys walk in and out. I'd even seen some girls. But
the places never tempted me. I really didn't know what
went on in them.

Well, I sure didn't want to go back to that cell. The mem-
ories of Sheila were still back there. And if I chose to go
back, I'd probably get a long, long sentence. These cops
would see to that. Why not take my chances with Uncle
Harvey? After all, as soon as I hit the street, I could take off
running. He'd never be able to catch me.

"Okay, you've painted the picture real clear," I said to the cops. "I'd be happy to work for Uncle Harvey."

No sooner had I said it, I realized something. Uncle Harvey must be a pimp! One thing I didn't want to do was work for a pimp. I'd known girls who were pimped. I'd always done it on my own and vowed I'd stay that way. Pimps were mean and ornery. If you didn't make as much money as they thought you should make, they'd kill you. And they'd take every penny you earned!

So when Harvey, all smiles, grabbed my arm, I pulled back and snapped. "No you don't! I'm not working for a dirty, filthy pimp!"

I didn't see his hand coming, or I would have ducked. It caught me on the cheek and sent me reeling across the room and sprawling on the floor. I jumped up, fists clenched, ready to tear into that fat, ugly pimp!

But the two cops anticipated my reaction and grabbed my arms. I was screaming and kicking and cursing, but that's all I could do. They held me securely.

"Cool it! Cool it!" one of them shouted. "Uncle Harvey is no pimp. We wouldn't let a pimp come in here and bail you out. Harvey owns a massage parlor where they give legit massages. Now don't blow it!"

I was furious, but I did manage to control my emotions a little better.

Harvey stomped his cigar butt into the floor and said, "Okay, Sid, forget this one. She's too mean and ornery. I don't want someone who blows up over every little thing. She'll drive all my customers away!"

"Wait a minute, Harvey," Sid pleaded. "Don't walk out on a good deal. This Valarie is going to be one of the best you've ever had. I just know it."

Sid sure seemed anxious for me to go with Harvey. And I

knew why. They wanted me out of jail before the investigation of Sheila's hanging started. If I didn't go along, I knew those two would really make it rough on me—probably get the judge to send me away for the rest of my life.

"Look at it this way, Harvey," Sid went on. "Last week you lost two girls to pimps. Evidently Valarie hates pimps. That's the kind you want in your business—pimp haters. You won't lose them to pimps. So this Valarie is really going to do great for you. I know it."

I guessed I'd better keep my mouth shut. Uncle Harvey was my ticket out of this place. And apparently he wasn't a pimp—that is, if I could believe these cops.

Trying to smooth things over, I said, "You're right! I do hate pimps. They beat up their girls. They cut up their girls. They throw their girls off of rooftops. So I'm glad to know Uncle Harvey's no pimp. I'd go to jail before I'd go off with some pimp. That's why I blew up. I'm sorry."

"Okay. I'll take you, then," Harvey said. "But so help me, if ever again you accuse me of being a pimp, I will do to you what you say those pimps do. I'll beat you and cut you and throw you off the rooftop! So let's get it straight: I hate pimps as much as you do!"

"You have to understand something about Uncle Harvey," Sid told me confidentially. "Every once in a while he comes in here and offers to help some poor girl out by giving her a job. But the pimps come after his girls, and there's a big war going on. Harvey has told us he's been threatened a few times. In fact, one pimp stabbed him in the arm. So you can understand why he hates to be called a pimp."

So that was it!

"Uncle Harvey," I said, squeezing his arm through his filthy topcoat, "please forgive me. I'll never use the word *pimp* around you again."

A big smile crossed his face as he said, "That's more like it. Now come along with me."

"Isn't there something I have to sign?" I asked.

"Well, Harvey's already taken care of most of the paperwork. All you have to do is sign this one here, and you're free to go. Just don't forget your court appearance, or Harvey forfeits the bond."

It seemed too simple. But I still planned to hit the street running. If Harvey tried to run after me, he'd likely keel over with a heart attack. This was going to be a piece of cake!

I signed the paper, but I sure wasn't planning to appear in court. So poor Harvey lost some money. So what?

Just before we went out the door, Harvey clamped his big hand around one of my arms. "Three months ago I bailed a girl out," he said. "Just as soon as we got to the sidewalk, she took off. So to prevent that, I'll just hold your arm. Okay?"

His fingers dug into my flesh. Maybe I could still break away, though.

A few steps from the police precinct, Harvey pulled his coat back enough to reveal a gun tucked into his belt. "See that, Valarie? That's further insurance that you don't take off running. You try to get away, and you'll end up with a bullet in your back. You understand?"

Now I was really worried. What had I gotten myself into?

We walked a couple of blocks and I asked, "How much farther to this joint of yours?"

Harvey bristled. "It's not a joint!" he corrected. "It's a massage parlor. Remember that—a massage parlor."

"Oh, I'm sorry," I said, realizing I'd better be very careful about what I said and how I said it. "Didn't Sid say it was the Blue Lagoon Massage Parlor? Is that it?"

"That's it," Harvey responded. "I like that name—Blue Lagoon. It's got class!"

I pulled my coat around me. It sure was cold this morning. What would it be like by tonight? I'd hate to be out hustling in weather like this.

Suddenly in the middle of the block I spotted the sign: BLUE LAGOON MASSAGE PARLOR.

It was just a hole in the wall. When we walked in, I noticed three girls sitting in a reception room. As soon as they saw Harvey, they snapped to attention.

"Valarie, I want you to meet Cindy, Martha, and Candi," Harvey said, pointing out each. "Girls, this is Valarie Lambert. She's our newest employee."

The three girls smiled and welcomed me cordially, but I noticed that their eyes mirrored fear. Was it really a legitimate business?

Harvey beckoned me down a hallway. Several little rooms lined the hallway, all looking about the same. He led me into one and pointed out the massage bench and table. It did look legitimate, but I still had my doubts.

Then he led me down to the end of the hall where he had his office. It was dirty and filthy—just like Harvey.

"Valarie, sit down," he said. "I'm going to have to—"

"For crying out loud, Harvey," I interrupted. "I don't know one thing about giving a massage. I never gave one in my whole life. I tried to tell you that in the station."

"Okay, okay, so you don't know how to give a massage," he replied. "But there are other things you know how to do."

"Like what?"

"You'll soon find out."

What was this dirty old man talking about? Would he give me a massage to demonstrate how it should be done? I didn't want his filthy hands roaming around on my body!

I hadn't had any drugs since last night, and suddenly the walls started to cave in on me. "Harvey," I said, "the cops probably didn't tell you this, but I've got a habit; and I'm getting sick now!"

Harvey grabbed his wastebasket, threw it toward me, and said, "Use that."

My stomach retched, and up came a bunch of green, slimy stuff.

I looked over at Harvey and said, "I'm sorry."

"Okay, let's see if I can get this straight," Harvey said. "Sid and Thomas seemed mighty anxious for me to take you. When I asked if you were a junkie, they said you weren't. They said you were out in the street hustling. So I said I'd bail you out. I wouldn't have done that if I had known. But now I don't have much choice, do I? You can't take back sale merchandise." Then he laughed uproariously at his little joke.

I was furious at those cops for not leveling with Harvey. And I was mad at Harvey. I wanted to scream at him to give me a bag of dope, but that would probably make him so mad that he'd kill me on the spot. I got the feeling that my life wasn't really worth all that much to him.

"How much of a run have you had?" Harvey asked.

"I've been on it for three months now. I've got a bad habit."

"Do you get off to get high, or do you get off to get straight?" he asked.

Harvey had been around. He knew the language.

"I get off just to get straight," I admitted.

Harvey reached into the bottom drawer of his desk and said, "I've got something for you, Valarie. I don't do this for every girl, but there is something about you I like. You've got spirit and spunk. Let's be friends from now on. Okay?"

What would Harvey be giving me? The only thing I needed was dope. But the owner of a massage parlor wouldn't have any dope around, would he? The cops said he ran a legitimate business.

Harvey threw something at me. As it slid across the desk, I immediately recognized it. It was the answer to my fondest dreams—a bag of dope!

I snatched it, almost feeling the surge of power as I held it in my hand.

Now all I needed was a set of works—nothing else, just works, and quickly!

"Harvey, thanks," I said. "I'll be your friend forever. You've got a set of works?"

"Not so fast, not so fast," he cautioned. "Yeah, I've got a set of works. But before I let you use them, we've got to agree on a couple of things."

At that stage I was ready to agree to almost anything—if I could just have that dope. As soon as it went coursing through my veins, I'd stop getting sick. I might even get a little high.

"Harvey, anything you say, baby. Anything."

He rubbed the stubble on his unshaved chin thoughtfully.

"Come on, Harvey, work the deal. Anything!"

"You really mean anything, Valarie?"

I squeezed the bag of dope in anticipation. "Harvey, let's not play games. You name it, and you can have it."

He leaned forward and asked, "Are you sure?"

I was ready to sell anything I had to get that set of works, even my body. It didn't matter what Harvey wanted, he was going to get it.

When he asked me again if I was sure, I couldn't wait any longer. The nerve endings of my arm were screaming for a fix. So I jumped up, ran around the desk, threw my arms around that slob, and kissed him like I'd never kissed a man before.

He threw his arms around me, and I realized for the first time how horrible he smelled. His breath stank. He'd probably never used a deodorant, and he probably hadn't bothered to bathe in weeks.

When I drew back, he said eagerly, "Let's do that again!"

All I could think of was that dope. I had to have it, regardless. So I threw my arms around Harvey and started kissing him passionately again. The stench was unbearable, but I had to have his set of works.

"Okay, Harvey," I said, backing away. "I've done my part; now you do yours."

He reached into another drawer. This time I was in a position where I could see the contents of that drawer. He must have had ten sets of works in there! Wow!

Before he had a chance to get his hand in the drawer, I reached in and grabbed a set. I suppose I should have asked him where he got them all. But right then I really didn't care. I had one of them in my hands.

"Got water?" I asked.

Harvey pointed. I rushed over, flung open the bathroom door, and unraveled the works. Harvey had it all there: the needle, the bottle cap, matches, everything! He might be fat and ugly, but at the moment in my eyes he was a darling. I'd be willing to kiss him anytime if he'd keep me in dope!

I quickly drilled myself. Then it hit me. My tenseness started to dissipate, and I began to float. It felt so good. Who cared about jail? Who cared about massage parlors? Who cared about dirty old Harvey? I'd got what I wanted out of life—dope!

I wandered back into his office and plopped into a chair. "How does it feel?" he asked me.

"Beautiful, Harvey, just beautiful! Those cops didn't tell me you were a drug dealer!"

Harvey leaped out of his chair and came toward me, his hand raised. Instinctively I covered my face for protection and yelled, "Harvey! Harvey! Listen to me. Man, I know you're no drug dealer. I was just kidding. I mean, Harvey, you're a great guy! You take good care of your employees. And, Harvey, I'll do anything you want me to. I mean, *anything!*"

I kept talking fast, hoping to talk him out of his plans to beat me up. I watched as he slowly dropped his fist.

"Baby, you've got your dope," Harvey said. "Now let's go to work."

I wasn't about to resist. If he'd supply my dope, I'd sure learn to massage.

He led me back to one of those little cubicles where he took off his shirt and jumped up on the table. "I'll teach you how to massage," he said, "but there are other things I can't teach you. You'll have to teach yourself those things."

"What do you mean?"

"Valarie, you are stupid. Don't you know what I mean?"

I sure didn't, and I was willing to admit it. But I had this sinking feeling that I'd soon find out!

4

"I hope you appreciate what I've done for you, Valarie," Harvey told me. "I've not only saved you from a long prison term, but I've also given you a bag of dope so you could get straight." Then he waggled his finger at me. "But I want to tell you something about your habit. Try to bring it down. Just because I gave you one bag doesn't mean I'm going to give you another."

Harvey had a mean look in his eyes. I wondered if he treated his girls well. Did he beat them? Would he beat me?

He flopped onto the bench and said, "Okay, give me a massage."

He was lying face down, so I started pushing on his back. It was the only thing I knew how to do.

"No, no! Not there!" he said disgustedly. "You start from the shoulders and work down."

So I started massaging the muscles around his neck.

"All right, now push harder," he ordered.

When I pushed harder, he yelled, "Not that hard, stupid!"

That really ticked me off. "Now hang on, Harvey!" I shouted. "I think you are fantastic for getting me out of jail. I'm ready to make you my dream man for giving me that bag of dope. But don't scream at me about massaging. I told you I didn't know from square one how to do this. Besides, my nerves are on edge!"

"All right, kid, just calm down. But if you want to have customers, you're going to have to develop a great technique."

"Listen, Harvey, the only technique I have developed is how to get drugs."

He turned his head toward me and smiled. "That's what I'm getting to, kid. Now listen."

He put his face back down on the bench and said, "Rub the muscles around my neck. After rubbing a couple of times, reach over and gently stroke my face. Pat my face twice."

I looked at him and realized he wasn't kidding. But when I hesitated, he said, "Come on now; do what I say. I'm going to teach you this technique. This will bring you in more money every time."

I really didn't want anything to do with this business. It made me feel kind of creepy. But I was interested in making money—because money meant dope. So I'd better do what Harvey told me to do.

I rubbed his neck muscles again and gently began to stroke his cheeks. I found his stubble loathsome, but I did it anyway, even patting his cheeks tenderly. He began to coo like a bird.

"Wow, that feels good!" he exclaimed. "You've got a good touch, kid. You're on the road."

He turned toward me again and said, "That was lesson number one. Now for lesson number two. Begin to work on the muscles right down the middle of my back toward my tailbone."

I knew this was coming—getting down to the lower part of his body, and I thought it was disgusting. But I still had to go through with it.

As I began to massage his back, he said, "Now stroke my side—gently—like you did my cheek."

When I began to stroke, Harvey cooed again. "That is just great!" he exclaimed. "You've got a real soft touch."

So far this business of massages wasn't too bad. At least Harvey was enjoying it, and I even felt a little better about it.

"Now rub near my tailbone and do some more stroking," Harvey ordered.

As I did what he had said, he began to coo again. Then he looked toward me and beamed. "I just know you are going to be my number-one massager!" he said. "I bet you are going to make lots of money. I mean, lots!"

"By the way, how do I charge for my services?" I asked. "Is there a standard fee?"

Harvey rolled over and sat up. "No," he answered. "The first thing I had to know was the kind of touch you had. If you have a soft touch, I can get a lot more for your services. You've got the touch, kid. So I think we can make a lot of money."

"How much?" I persisted.

"That depends. If you can do a quick, thorough job and get the customer satisfied, you'll be able to do six or seven a night."

"Seven a night? That sounds like a lot. How long does a massage take?"

Harvey smiled knowingly. "Like I say, kid, it all depends."

"Okay, but how much do I charge?" I demanded, getting somewhat exasperated with the runaround I was getting.

"Our basic charge is fifteen dollars," Harvey responded.

"Only fifteen dollars?" I shot back. "If I do six, that's ninety bucks. That doesn't sound like I'm making a lot of money!"

"I know; you're going to tell me you made more than that out on the street."

"You'd better believe I did. I'd usually make three hundred dollars a night. Man, I've made as high as a thousand bucks a night!"

"Valarie, Valarie, don't lie to me!" he said patronizingly. "I know you used to hang out on Forty-second Street. You never made a thousand bucks a night there!"

"Don't sell me short, Harvey," I said. "I did one night. Two guys each paid me three hundred bucks at the Waldorf Astoria. And I got four other guys who paid me a hundred each. I'm a first-class girl. If I didn't have this drug habit, I'd be a millionaire."

Harvey grunted, "Ha! You're just like all the other junkies. You spend it as fast as you get it!"

I wanted to slap him. Oh, how I hated to be called a junkie. But there was no denying I was one!

"Well, if that's the way you feel about me, I'm leaving," I announced. "I don't—"

"You're what?" Harvey said in mock surprise. "Did I hear you correctly? Did you say you're leaving?"

I knew he carried a gun. He'd be the type to shoot me in the back if I tried to get away.

"Well, maybe not right this minute," I said lamely. "But I'm going to tell you something, Harvey. You'd better treat me right."

Harvey was on his feet and lit into me. He grabbed my blouse and jerked me toward him, snarling, "You little twerp! I should have let you rot in jail! You're just like all the rest of the girls. No matter what I do for you, you're never satisfied! Listen, Valarie, you've got a short memory. You've got to remember all I did for you. I took you out of that stinking jail. I gave you a bag of dope. And now you're already getting smart with me. I ought to take you back to that jail. This time they'd lock you up and throw away the key!"

He was twisting my blouse so hard it was pulling against my neck. If I had wanted to, I could have jerked my knee up and hit him. That would fix him. But I worried about that gun.

I tried to squirm loose, but that didn't work. Finally in desperation I said, "Okay, I'm sorry! I'm sorry! I appreciate all you've done for me. I'll stay here as long as you want me, Harvey."

He relaxed his grip, and I breathed easier. I knew it would be folly to cross this guy up. He'd kill me without batting an eyelash. He'd probably done it before!

Without warning he shoved me, and I went hurtling across the room, banging my head against the wall.

"What was that for?" I demanded, glaring at him.

"That was to teach you a little lesson. I really should have knocked your head against the wall and hit you a few times," he said. "You're lucky, Valarie. I don't allow my girls to give me any lip."

I never was the kind to take abuse sitting down. I looked at Harvey. He was old and fat and out of shape. I'd knocked a couple of perverts around. I could take on Harvey.

I clenched my fist, ready to smack him in the mouth. Then I'd—

He must have noticed the murder in my eye because he screamed, "Angelo! Angelo!"

I heard heavy footsteps shaking the walls. Then the door burst open, and there stood the biggest giant of a man I'd ever seen anywhere. He looked like a gorilla—huge, ugly, and weighing at least three hundred pounds. And he stood almost seven feet tall!

"Duh, what do you want, boss?"

I could tell his IQ was on the down side of sixty.

Harvey just pointed to me, and Angelo came toward me, shoulders hunched, arms extended. I realized I was soon going to feel like the suitcase in that TV commercial where a gorilla gives the suitcase a mauling!

"Don't you touch me!" I yelled with more bravery than I felt at that moment.

Angelo's hands surrounded my waist, and he lifted me up, banging my head against the ceiling. I was kicking and screaming, and Angelo was laughing at my plight.

"What now, boss?" he asked, looking toward Harvey but still holding me high in the air. "Can I break her arm now?"

Harvey was grinning. And I realized the kind of situation I was in. I was a captive in Harvey's zoo. There was no way I could get out!

"Let me down! Let me down!" I kept screaming. "I didn't mean any harm!"

Harvey stood there grinning; Angelo kept growling. I almost spit at both of them, but I knew I'd end up with a broken arm or leg if I tried something that stupid!

"Come on, Harvey!" I yelled. "I got the message. I promise I won't get smart again! Now call off your gorilla!"

It seemed as though I was up there for an eternity, but finally Harvey, still grinning, said, "Okay, Angelo, put the little girl down."

Angelo slowly lowered me to the floor, still glaring at me and saying menacingly, "Last girl is still in a cast; I broke her back!"

I shuddered. This ape could easily do that!

Harvey's grin turned to an extremely serious expression as he said, "You've learned your lesson, Valarie? Like I say, just button that fat lip of yours!"

I nodded eagerly. I wasn't about to make waves now!

"Angelo, go back to your room," Harvey ordered. "But keep your ears open. If this kid gets smart, I'll call you again. Then you can break her leg."

"Yeah, boss, whatever you say!" Angelo replied, rubbing his hands together in gleeful anticipation. "I'll tear her limb from limb!"

The utter terror of the situation was sinking in. Maybe I'd have been better off to have taken my chances in jail!

After Angelo left, Harvey stood there, hands on his hips, telling me, " I'm sorry I had to do that to you. Some of the girls who come here to work are nice and sweet. Others are mean and ornery. But when I introduce them to Angelo, they get the message—just like you did!"

"I got the message, Harvey! You can trust me now. And I really appreciate what you've done for me."

I really didn't know if I did appreciate it or not, but I wasn't about to argue the point at this time.

"Now back to business," Harvey said, apparently satisfied with my contriteness. "Like I said, the basic charge for the massage is fifteen bucks. Anything you get beyond fifteen, we split fifty-fifty. You know what I mean?"

"You mean if a guy comes in and I charge him twenty-five dollars, I have to give you the first fifteen, and we split the extra ten; I get five bucks and you get five bucks. Right?"

"Right. You got it, kid."

"Wrong!" I responded. "That doesn't make sense. I thought you said I was going to make fifteen dollars a massage. Now you're saying I don't get anything unless I charge extra. How come?"

"Ever hear of overhead?" Harvey said, laughing. "It costs me a bundle to keep this place open—rent, lights, heat, a place for you girls to live. And there are people I've got to pay to keep me alive. I've got to have that first fifteen bucks."

"What you're trying to tell me is that if a guy comes in and pays me fifteen bucks, you get it all, and I don't get a dime?"

"You've got it, kid."

"That's not fair, Harvey" I exploded. "You got me out of jail to make a slave out of me! It's not fair! It's not fair!"

When Harvey raised his arm, I thought he was going to call for Angelo. That made me shut up in a hurry!

"Okay, Valarie, we've played games long enough," Harvey said. "You're either terribly naive or just plain stupid. When these guys come in here, they're wanting more than a massage. And that's where you get the opportunity to make a lot of money."

I stared at Harvey. The message was beginning to sink in. This massage parlor was a front for a house of prostitution!

"You're trying to tell me that if a guy wants more than a massage, just give him everything he wants?"

Harvey nodded.

"That's beneath my dignity!" I exploded again. "I don't care who the guy is; I'm not selling my body for a measly fifteen dollars!"

"Come on, Valarie," Harvey cajoled. "You've got to be smarter than that. For fifteen bucks the guy gets a massage—and that's all. You give him a massage he'll never forget. Then at the end of the massage, you ask if there is anything else you can do for him. Nine times out of ten the guys won't even wait for you to ask the question. All you have to do is quote a price for the extra services, and they'll give it to you. I mean, they'll give you whatever you ask for!"

"Let's go over this again," I said. "I give the guy a massage for fifteen bucks. When I get near the end of the massage and the guy is getting frisky, I tell him for another hundred bucks, I can do that. Is that it?"

Harvey beamed. "Exactly! If you're smart, you'll ask for two hundred. Then you'll make a hundred, and I'll make a hundred. It's that simple. And let me tell you something. My place has a good reputation, so I've got a lot of steady customers. That's to your advantage, Valarie. It beats standing out on the street. And I think with your touch, you'll have a lot of repeats."

So that was it. This really *was* a house of prostitution.

"Sounds to me like you're a glorified pimp," I said, without thinking.

"I told you never to say that word around me!" Harvey snarled. "You want me to call Angelo again?"

I backed away and yelled, "No! No! Let's not get into that again!"

"Valarie, I'm no pimp," Harvey said. "I don't believe in that. I don't beat my girls. Sure, I've got Angelo to keep them in line. But that's not the main reason he's here. Occasionally we get perverts in here who try to hurt our girls. Now, Valarie, get this straight. If anyone tries anything out of line, all you've got to do is yell for Angelo. He'll come rushing in and rip the maniac apart. So Angelo is here mostly for your protection. You don't have to worry about someone hurting you."

I hadn't thought about that advantage. When I was on the street, I was strictly on my own, and I'd gotten myself into some real scrapes a time or two. In those hotel rooms a pervert could murder you, and no one would know, or care. I lived with the fear that any guy I took could be a pervert. You couldn't always tell by the way they looked or dressed. So I guess it was worth something to have Angelo as protection.

"I want to tell you something else, Valarie," Harvey went on. "I run a legitimate business here. I'm doing these men a real service. Businessmen come to New York City from all over. They're tense from all the pressures of their business. So they come in here and get a nice massage that relaxes away those tensions. Well, they're away from their wives, so they get a little extra. Nobody gets hurt. So we are performing a service—a voluntary service to people who are willing to pay for it. Some of these guys are willing to pay a bundle. There's nothing the matter with that. After all, we are performing a service."

I didn't argue with him. I'd used the same rationalization myself when I was on the street. Besides, I really didn't care about the morals or ethics of the business. All I was interested in was that I was going to be able to make some money, and with the money I could buy dope. I didn't know yet where I'd get the dope, but I'd figure that out later.

"Up on the second floor you'll have your own room," Harvey went on. "You'll have to share the bathroom with the other girls. But it's a roof over your head. Think of it, Valarie. Remember how cold it is out there on Times Square. You won't have to go out and hustle. You'll make your money right here—in comfort. You'll be warm. And you've got Angelo to protect you from the perverts. Me and Angelo will take care of you forever!"

I didn't like the way he said *forever*. But I really didn't expect to live long. My drug habit would probably end in an overdose, or somebody would get me. I'd seen it happen too many times to girls I knew—girls like Sheila.

Sheila! I hadn't thought of her since I'd got out of jail! She was the real reason I was here. Those cops didn't want me to tell what I knew about that situation. Maybe if. . . .

That thought was interrupted by some man screaming in the next room. I started toward the door, but Harvey pushed me back with, "Don't worry. That's Candi in there with one of our regulars, Sherwin Ackerman. He likes a special technique."

"Yeah, but why does he scream? Is he hurting? Does Candi know what she's doing?"

Harvey laughed. "Of course Candi knows what she's doing! That's just something that Mr. Ackerman likes."

"You mean he's getting a little frisky, and—"

"No, no, no!" Harvey replied. "He's not that kind of guy. He's got a wife and three kids at home, and he's true blue."

"But why is he screaming?"

"Well, you'd almost have to see what's happening in there," Harvey told me. "It's hard to describe."

"You mean I can go in and watch?" I said, starting for the door again.

"Heavens, no!" Harvey yelled. "Don't do that! Whenever a door is closed, that door is *closed*. These men want privacy. You must understand and respect that. What goes on in any room is absolutely private!"

"So if a guy wants to scream, I just let him scream?"

"Valarie, whenever a guy gets into your room, you give him whatever he wants. I mean, whatever. You don't have to worry about getting hurt because all you've got to do is yell for Angelo, and he'll come running. He's your protection."

I nodded. I understood that part.

"Now every so often a guy will come in who wants something different," Harvey went on. "And let me tell you that these guys who want other things are always willing to pay a big price—maybe three hundred dollars. So it's an easy way to make extra money."

"I think I'm beginning to catch on," I told him. "Whatever a guy wants, I'm supposed to give it to him—for a price. Right?

Harvey grinned and nodded.

"Look, Harvey, I may be a prostitute, but I'm not perverted," I protested. "I'm just not into that kind of stuff. I mean, I think it's thoroughly disgusting. If some guy asks me to do things I just can't do, then I'm not going to go through with it. I'm sorry, but I've still got my dignity."

"Come on, Valarie, none of my girls are perverted. I'm not into that either. Those perverts hang out around Forty-second Street. You can get the creeps down there to do anything for a price. But not in my place. Like I say, I run a respectable business. I've never once asked any of my girls to get into any kind of perversion. All I'm trying to say is that some of these guys are just a little bit different in what they like and want. So just go along with it. And, believe me, it's not perversion. You'll see."

"If it's not perversion, what is it?" I pressed.

"Well, like I said, it's difficult to describe in words. Just remember, whatever they want, you give it to them—for a price. Don't do anything for free. Always name a price. And make it high enough to get the dough for you and me. Okay?"

"You're sure it's not perversion?"

Harvey shook his head firmly. "No, it's not perversion. I assure you of that."

Now he really had me wondering. It sure sounded like perversion. Harvey wouldn't tell me what it actually was.

Well, I soon found out!

5

Harvey explained to me that the room in which we were talking would be mine exclusively for work.

"Can I decorate it a little—like put up some pictures?" I asked.

"Don't get cute, Valarie," Harvey growled. "This is a business place. We don't want men staring at pictures."

I looked around and noticed a bunch of dots on the far wall—all kinds of black dots on the white wall. They really looked out of place. If that was Harvey's idea of decoration, I wanted to set him straight.

"What's the deal on those black dots?" I asked.

"None of your business!" he snapped.

"What?" I responded. "You told me this was my room. Seems as though I ought to be able to ask about those dots on the wall. I really don't care for them, and—"

"You want me to call Angelo again?" Harvey interrupted. "Your lip is starting to get fat."

One thing I didn't want was Angelo. "Okay, okay, you can have your stupid dots! They just looked strange and made me wonder. That's all."

"You've got to learn to shut up, Valarie," Harvey told me. "You ask too many questions. We'll get along a lot better if you learn to keep your mouth shut."

I just shrugged. Maybe I did ask too many questions. That always seemed to be second nature to me. I had to know why. Besides, this whole setup made me nervous.

"Come with me," Harvey said, reaching for my hand. "You'll sit out front with the other girls until someone asks for you or until your turn comes up."

I followed obediently, wondering if I had learned all I needed to know. But it was getting so I was really afraid to ask anything. Every time I opened my mouth, I was getting threatened with Angelo!

Martha and Cindy were in the reception room. I guessed Candi was still with that customer. Harvey pointed toward a lounge chair and ordered gruffly, "Sit!"

I felt as though he were giving orders to his dog, but I meekly obeyed. Cindy and Martha smiled at me. They seemed content. I wondered if they were as nice as they looked, or were they mean and ornery?

Harvey started explaining the procedure. "When a guy walks in, he may ask for Cindy, Martha, Candi, or even you, Valarie. The whole secret is to build up a trade. Some guys come in every night, some once a week. But the girls all have some regular customers. And we want you to build up your regular trade, too. Right, girls?"

They nodded rather mechanically—almost like puppets. So he wanted me to build up a trade? I didn't plan to be here that long. I didn't get sprung from one prison to get stuck in another one! I was going to be my own woman!

"Who's next?" Harvey asked.

"I am," Martha answered.

"Okay, then Cindy, and then Valarie," Harvey said. With that he walked back to his office.

My heart beat faster. I wondered what my first customer would be like. I had to be able to make enough to get dope!

Before long the front door opened, and two guys walked in. Martha and Cindy stood, so I did, too. I guess maybe the guys wanted to look over the merchandise.

They were really giving us the once over. One pointed to Cindy, and the other toward me. Cindy smiled big, so I did, too; I knew how to do that!

As I took the guy to my room, I tried to make conversation. "Kind of cold out there, isn't it?"

"Man, it sure is!" he exclaimed. "That's why I figured a massage might warm me up. Are you in the warming-up business?"

This was easier than I thought. "I've got the hottest room in New York City!" I said, smiling beguilingly.

I shut the door behind us, and he climbed up on the table and started taking off his shirt. I gave him a massage, remembering what Harvey had said about stroking his cheek and the other parts of his body. By the time I got through with the massage, the guy was jumping up and down.

When we tried to work a deal, we haggled on the price. He insisted he'd never paid over fifty dollars before. In fact, he said that Martha only charged him fifty dollars. So I figured maybe I was being a little too greedy and agreed to the fifty dollars. At least I could get a bag of dope with my share of the profits.

He paid me fifty dollars, and in a few minutes it was all over.

As soon as the guy walked out, Harvey walked in.

"How did it go?" he asked.

"Well, just so-so. I only got fifty bucks from that scrooge."

"Oh, I should have told you," Harvey replied. "That was Bill Samuels. He never pays more than fifty bucks."

"That's what he told me," I returned. "He said that

Martha only charged him fifty bucks. I didn't know whether he was telling the truth or not."

"Yeah, I think he was with Martha last time," Harvey said. "Bill trades off. But he does come in regularly—at least once a week. But it's always a maximum of fifty bucks. I guess we should have tipped you off."

"When do I get my cut?" I asked.

"Hey, you're really greedy, aren't you?" Harvey said. "You get paid when I pay you. It's as simple as that."

"Come on, Harvey. You said you treated your girls right. Just so I can settle my own mind, when do I get paid?"

"When we close tonight. So don't get anxious. Go out there and get another customer."

I wasn't sure I could trust Harvey. But I didn't have much choice—especially with Angelo poised back there ready to pounce on me for the slightest infraction of Harvey's rules! Then something else struck me. How did Harvey know how much I got with each customer? Maybe later on I could rip him off by not telling the truth about how much I charged!

When I walked back to the reception room, no one was there. Cindy, Martha, and Candi all must be busy. Harvey must really be raking in the dough on this place!

Then another guy walked in, looked me over, and asked, "Are you new?"

I nodded.

"You've got lots of experience?" he asked.

"Do I have experience?" I returned. "I've been doing this since I was thirteen! I've really got great experience!"

"You'll do," he told me, almost condescendingly.

We walked back to my room, and it was the same process all over again. The massage part was almost incidental. This was, in fact, a house of prostitution. But it sure beat going to a sleazy hotel with all the rats and roaches and filth—and perverts! And I had Angelo for protection. Some of the girls I used to know had pimps for protection, but this arrangement beat that!

Well, that night I had four customers and took in four hundred dollars above the cost of the massages. About two in the morning Harvey paid me two hundred dollars, and I went up to my room.

I realized that I really had a problem. I had to get off again, or I was going to be sick. How would I get out of here to get some dope?

I flopped onto my bed to think. It wasn't really a bed—just a cot with a thin, lumpy mattress over some springs. But it was better than those benches in the jail cells. And it was a place to think! At least I was alone.

I heard the three girls laughing in one of the rooms down the hall. Since they were occupied, maybe I could escape!

Cautiously, quietly opening my door, I looked both ways. Good! Nobody around. I edged down the hall and started down the steps. They creaked and groaned, but I didn't worry too much. I figured Harvey was gone, and the girls were making so much noise that they wouldn't hear me.

I made it safely to the bottom of the stairs, down the hall past the little rooms where we girls worked, and up to the reception room. But when I got there I was in for a big surprise! In the dim light I could make out that incredible ape, Angelo.

"Going somewheres?" he asked menacingly.

I had to get out of this one, or he'd tear me apart!

"Oh, it's you down here," I said, acting as though I was greatly relieved. "I'm new and don't know all the procedures. I figured you and Harvey went home at night. Well,

I heard this noise down here and thought somebody was breaking in to try to rip Harvey off. So I came down to check things out."

"Valarie, you don't worry," Angelo told me firmly. "Me, Angelo, take care of this place. I live here, too. Me, I like to fight. Me, I like to hurt people. No one will rip off Harvey while Angelo is around. And me, I take care of you, too."

So help me, I've never seen anyone who looked so much like a gorilla. And when he started toward me, I backed up. I wasn't sure what he might have on his mind!

"Don't be scared," he said softly. "Angelo not afraid down here. Me, I take care of you."

As he got closer, my heart beat faster. After all, he was a man, even though he looked like a gorilla. Did he expect free favors in return for taking care of us girls? I knew it would be absolutely useless to try to resist. I'd better play it his way.

I moved up and threw my arms around his waist, hugging him tight. "Angelo, I love you very much," I lied. "Thank you for taking care of me."

He patted my back, almost tenderly, it seemed. I was hoping he wouldn't squeeze me. He could crush me just being nice!

I drew back and looked up—way up—into his eyes. The ape was absolutely melting. I stroked his cheek, and he was really starting to respond.

"Now, Angelo, I've got to get back to my room and go to sleep so I'll be ready to work for Harvey tomorrow," I said. "And I'll sleep a lot better, knowing that I'm safe, knowing that you are down here taking care of me."

Angelo backed away. I really started to feel sorry for him. I didn't know where he came from or how he ended up here. Who knew? Maybe Harvey had bailed him out of jail. But it made me mad to think that Harvey was exploiting him, too—just as he was exploiting us girls. And there wasn't much we could do about it. I had thought of escaping. But right now that was out of the question. I'd have to find another way out. But even more pressing right now was my need for some dope.

Back at the top of the stairs I heard the girls still laughing and carrying on. Wondering what they were doing, I knocked on the door and asked, "Can the new girl come in?"

"Sure," someone yelled.

When I opened the door, I saw the three of them all seated on the bed, laughing, giggling, and acting as though they were having the time of their lives.

"Want to get off?" Candi asked.

I couldn't believe that question. Harvey had said he frowned on his girls taking dope. Were these girls on dope, and he didn't know it? I sure wasn't going to tell!

"Candi just got off," Martha said. "You want to buy some dope?"

"Do I? Wow! Why didn't you tell me you had some up here? I mean, man, I've been in my room, wondering how I was going to get out to get some dope. Of course I want to get off."

Martha reached under the mattress, pulled out a bag of dope, and said, "That'll be twenty-five bucks."

That was more than I paid on the street, but I couldn't get out to the street. So I handed her a twenty and a five and said, "Thanks, Martha. Have you got works I can borrow?"

"Yes and no," Martha replied. "I've got works, but not that you can borrow. But you can use them for another twenty-five bucks."

Martha sounded exactly like a dope dealer! When I argued that I just wanted to borrow them this one time, she said, "Look, I don't know anything about you. Maybe you've got hepatitis. I can't take a chance on just letting you use the needle."

She was right, of course. Junkies did share needles—and it was one of the worst things you could do. But sometimes you were so desperate that you just didn't care.

Martha reached under the mattress again and pulled out a set of works. I was in no position to argue and handed her twenty-five dollars.

Candi let me use her cooker, and I got off. It felt just tremendous.

When I noticed Cindy and Martha just watching me, I asked, "What's the matter? Aren't you girls going to get off?"

"Naw, we drink a little, but Martha and I aren't into dope," Cindy told me.

So Martha sold the stuff but didn't use it? She must be smarter than I gave her credit for being. And I hoped Cindy had enough sense to stay off the needle. How I wished I'd never started. If people only knew the hell it would lead to!

"Does Harvey know about this?" I asked.

Candi laughed. "Naw, he thinks we're straight."

"Yeah, but suppose he finds out?"

"No problem," Candi responded. "We've got so much dirt on this guy that he wouldn't dare turn us in. I mean, this place is a den of iniquity."

"Yeah, but it's a good living for us," Cindy interrupted. "I used to be a secretary making one hundred and fifty dollars a week. Now I make that much a night and get free room! I mean, it's a great job."

"But you've got to be smart about it," Martha interjected. "I imagine one of these days Harvey will fail to pay off somebody, and we'll have a raid. I mean, a real raid."

"I wouldn't worry too much," Cindy responded. "Harvey is smart. He keeps his tracks covered. One night I saw a couple of guys from the vice squad walk in, look around, and walk out. In fact, one guy opened my door, when I was in there with this guy and we were going at it. He could have busted me right then, but he acted as though he didn't see a thing. That's why I say Harvey must be covering his tracks because that guy didn't bust us."

Candi sat there nodding and telling me it was a great place to work. I guess she was a lot like me. It really didn't matter too much as long as she got her dope.

"If it's such a great place to work, how come Harvey won't let me hang some pictures on the wall in my room?" I asked. "I mean, all it's got are those ugly black dots—"

Candi started to laugh. "You've got black dots in your room?" she asked, acting as though the whole thing was hilarious.

"Yeah, man. I've got those dots."

"I've got news for you, Valarie," she said. "I've got dots, too—little dots, big dots, middle-sized dots."

She sat there nodding and giggling. What was so funny?

"Will Harvey let you put pictures on your wall?" I asked.

"No, man. No pictures. Just black dots. Right, Cindy?"

I looked at Cindy and asked, "You've got black dots in your room, too?"

Cindy nodded. I looked at Martha.

"I've got them, too," she said.

By this time all three of them were laughing and giggling. What was so funny about those dots?

"Did you take a close look at those dots in your room?" Candi asked.

"No, I just noticed them there and thought how ugly

they were. I figured maybe it was Harvey's idea of decoration. He's got about as much taste as a pig. Besides, he got
upset when I mentioned them and threatened to call in
Angelo. I didn't want that ape manhandling me!"

Candi stood up and motioned for me to follow. "I want
to show you something," she said.

I went with her down the hall, down the creaking stairs. I
wondered if we'd run into Angelo.

Sure enough, when we got into the hallway, he was
standing at the far end, watching us.

"Angelo, my sweet darling," Candi called, running toward him. "It's time for another kiss!"

He threw his arms open wide, and she jumped into them.
He lifted her up, and she really kissed him. He let out a war
whoop. He really got something out of that!

When he put her down, she came back to me and whispered, "I've got Angelo set up. If Harvey ever crosses me,
I'm going to yell for Angelo and tell him to kill Harvey.
Angelo loves me, and he'll do anything for me because his
love is so intense. You just wait and see."

Candi was smart! I'd already had some experience in
leading Angelo on. I'd play up to him so that next time he'd
slam Harvey's head into the ceiling, not mine!

"Angelo, darling, we're just going to check out Valarie's
room a minute," Candi called. "She's new here, you
know."

Angelo smiled and blew me a kiss. I blew one back at
him. He seemed so pleased that I did it.

Inside my room Candi turned on the light and pointed to
the wall. "Go over and take a close look at those dots," she
said.

I stared at them. They just looked like different-sized
black dots on a white wall.

"Come on, Candi, don't put me on," I said. "They're just dots. That's all."

"Take another look."

I got right up next to the dots, even rubbing my hands over them. The only difference I could see was that they were different sizes.

When I turned questioningly toward Candi, she said disgustedly, "Valarie, you're really stupid. Look! Look!"

This time I practically had my nose on them as I looked. Still nothing.

"Please don't call me stupid," I said. "But all I see are black dots of different sizes."

"Look at that one just above your head."

I glanced up, puzzled. When I started reaching toward it, Candi said, "The one just to the right of your hand now."

That dot looked just like all the others. But when I rubbed my hand over it, I realized it was glass.

"Hey, you're right!" I exclaimed. "That one is different. It's glass. How come?"

"I called you stupid once," Candi said. "Now I'm going to have to call you stupid again. You mean you've got no idea what that is?"

I shook my head. But as I thought about it, I realized somebody could watch me through it. Probably it was a one-way mirror.

"Ah, I get it!" I exclaimed. "Old Uncle Harvey gets his jollies by watching what goes on in here. Right?"

"Not quite, Valarie. It's more than that. You'll never believe what Harvey is up to."

"Listen, I'd believe almost anything about Harvey," I responded. "What's he up to?"

"Come on," she said, reaching for my hand and leading me to another room, sort of a storage room. When she turned on the light, I saw a small TV camera sitting up on a shelf, with the lens pointing in toward the wall.

"What kind of a setup is this?" I asked.

"You must come from a mental institution!" Candi sighed, exasperated. "Don't you know what's going on?"

"I'm sorry, but I don't," I replied. "Tell me."

"That TV camera is lined up with that piece of glass in your room," she said. "When a guy comes into your room, Harvey turns on this TV camera and takes pictures of you and that guy making out."

"What?" I yelled. "You mean that dirty Harvey is taking pictures of me and those guys in that room?"

Candi nodded. "That's exactly what he's doing."

I was furious. "Why would he do that?" I demanded.

"Valarie, Harvey's a smart dude. He's got two big reasons for making those videotapes. First, if some guy tries to give him a bad time, he can use that tape to blackmail the guy. But more than that, he takes these and sells them to the porno shops on Forty-second Street."

"He does what?" I yelled. "You mean he takes pictures of me and those guys and sells them to porno shops?"

"You're getting the picture," Candi said, laughing.

"That's illegal!" I shouted.

Candi snickered. I guess she had a right to. Nothing about this place was legal!

"Well, Harvey has no right to do something like that!" I fumed. "I didn't agree to appear in any porno films for a bunch of perverts to watch. Besides, one of those guys who comes in here might end up buying the film and finding himself in it. Then Harvey will really wind up with a lawsuit on his hands."

Candi hee-hawed at that suggestion. "Sure! Sure! she said. "That guy will have the tape played in the courtroom so the jury can see the evidence. Can you imagine how that will go over if the guy is married or has a good job? No way is any guy in his right mind going to threaten to sue over something like that. There's no way he can afford to do it! Harvey's got nothing to worry about."

"But it's indecent!" I countered. "How could Harvey be so dirty as to pull something like that on me?"

"Not just on you, honey. He's got a setup like this for each room. Look at it this way. You can be a big TV star!"

She saw a tear trickle down my cheek and came over and put her arm around me. "Valarie, you've got to get used to guys like Harvey. They'll do anything to make a buck. He's got a great thing going, and he's going to keep it going. All those dots in your room are there to camouflage the one important dot—the one the camera shoots through. People don't know they're being filmed. They just come in here and do their thing. Harvey makes money on that, and he makes even more on the videotapes."

I couldn't believe it. These massage parlors might look rather innocent, but inside was all sorts of intrigue!

Then I remembered that guy I'd heard screaming when Candi was in the next room with him. "Hey, I heard you with some guy who was making quite a racket. What was that all about?"

"I tell you, that'll be great on film!" Candi responded. "But I can't tell you what it was."

"Why not? Why is everybody so secretive about what goes on around here?"

"You'll find out for yourself," Candi told me.

And the next night I did!

6

I was still asleep the following morning when Candi knocked on my door and asked if I wanted to go get some breakfast. I realized I was quite hungry. Besides, I needed to be up and around looking for a supplier of dope. Would Martha sell me more?

Candi took me to a nearby coffee shop. It felt good to be away from the Blue Lagoon. Maybe I could find a way so I wouldn't have to go back!

Candi must have been reading my thoughts, for she said, "Valarie, let's make a deal. It's my responsibility to keep tabs on you for a week. After that, you'll be able to go out and get your meals by yourself."

"Ha!" I snorted. "This is worse than a prison!"

"Don't get huffy!" Candi shot back. "It's just a policy that Harvey has. The first week you're on probation. After all, Harvey did bail you out, and he had to put up a lot of money, I bet. If you jump bail, Harvey's stuck. So he's taken a chance on you, Valarie. He's just watching out for his investment. You understand that, don't you?"

"Don't talk to me about understanding!" I said. "Harvey stands to make a lot of money on me—with those video-tapes and all. Besides, he could do more than give us half of what we make."

77

"Hey, don't knock it," Candi cut in. "We do all right. And get out of that pretty little head of yours any idea of wandering off. If you go, Harvey will beat me up. He might even sic Angelo on me. And someday, somewhere I'd find you. I'd have Angelo with me, and it would be tough on you!"

"Is that why you make love to Angelo?"

"Well, let's just call it insurance," she said. "If I ever need Angelo, I know he'll be on my side. And if you take off, he and I will turn this town upside down until we find you. And good old Angelo will do anything I tell him to do. When he gets through with you, you'll never be able to walk again. You understand?"

I wished she wouldn't be so harsh. I was looking for a friend, not a keeper!

After breakfast she asked me if I wanted to do some shopping.

"Sure do," I responded. "I came here in such a hurry that I didn't bring anything with me. When that cop busted me, he didn't let me go back to my apartment and pack a suitcase."

Candi laughed. "I know how that is," she said. "I used to work for a pimp. But one day I got busted, and Uncle Harvey bailed me out. I figured it was a good way to get away from that dirty pimp. He used to beat me. I've been here a year now."

"But what about getting dope?" I asked. That was always the most important thing to me. "Do we keep on getting it from Martha? Where does she get it?"

"Well, after you've been here a week, you can get out and make your own contacts on the street if you want to—just so Harvey doesn't find out. But I buy mine from Martha because it's safer. Oh, it costs a little more, but I don't run the risk of buying from some undercover cop or getting a hot shot or anything like that. Martha gets good dope. She's got this guy who comes in every other day for a massage. He's a pusher. Now don't try to muscle in on him, Valarie. He's Martha's customer. The guy's name is Robert Sandelman. He looks like a businessman carrying a brief-case. But in his case he carries dope. That's who she buys her stuff from. Martha knows you're hooked. I'm sure she'll get enough from him so she can continue to sell you some. I think it's safest and best to buy from her because we can do it up in our rooms—and Harvey doesn't need to know about it."

Maybe this place wasn't so bad after all. I'd make enough money to buy my dope and could shoot up and get high. And I wouldn't have to worry all the time about get-ting busted.

"Okay, I hear you," I told her. "I won't try to muscle in on Martha's Mr. Sandelman. And I'll buy my dope from her for now anyway."

Candi took me to a boutique where I bought a couple of pairs of jeans, some blouses, and some underclothes. She also guided me to a place where I could buy a set of works. Now I was almost out of money. I had to save twenty-five dollars for a bag of dope—or I'd really be in trouble.

Back at the massage parlor I bought the dope from Martha and got off. We just sat around nodding that after-noon. Harvey said we didn't have to start work until four. Cindy and Martha had been working since noon. Ap-parently there wasn't a lot of business until later in the day, so we girls worked shifts.

A little before four I walked downstairs to have a chat with Harvey. I wanted to have some kind of an under-standing about that TV camera.

When I walked into his office, he was sitting behind his desk, his cigar pouring fumes into the air. When he saw me, he stood and said, "Valarie, my little sweetie! How did it go last night? Get a good sleep? Been having a good time today?"

"Yeah, I slept like a baby," I said.

"I was just talking to Candi about you," he went on. "She says you're one of the best girls we've had. She said you're obedient, understanding, tender, and you know how to make money. Perfect combination."

"Yeah," I said. "I understand Candi's my warden and has to monitor every move I make."

"Well, it's not quite like that," Harvey said. "But if I said you could come and go as you please, I suspect you'd be the type to go and never come back. Right?"

Without waiting for me to respond, he went on. "I used to play the game that way, but I learned my lesson. Two girls jumped bail. I had to send Angelo after them. He may seem dumb, but he stays on the trail of a girl like a bloodhound. He found them—poor girls. I never did ask him what he did with them." Harvey laughed as though it was terribly funny.

"Harvey, I'm not like that," I told him. "You can trust me. Really you can. I don't need Candi."

"You don't understand, Valarie," he said. "Trust isn't something I give. Trust is something you earn. So after you've been around a week, then we'll try you on your own. But if you bust loose after that, I'm still sending Angelo after you. He'll find you and teach you a lesson you'll never forget."

"Yeah, Candi warned me about that," I said. "I'm not about to have my head busted by that ape."

"Well, I just want you to know that if you jump bail,

you'll be in big trouble," Harvey told me. "You've got to go back to court in a couple of months, but I'll be working on that. In the meantime, don't try taking off!"

He made it pretty clear that I'd be in real trouble if I tried to get away. So I decided to get to the subject I had come in to talk to him about.

"Been to any good movies lately?" I asked.

"No, I don't have time for those junky things," he replied. "When I go to a movie, I think about what goes on behind the scenes. I mean, like the one with that guy walking across the desert all alone? I know there are fifty people there with him. It's all a fantasy, and I just can't get into movies."

Harvey was either dense or he didn't want to talk about what I was getting at.

"I mean, have you ever thought about movies in this place?" I asked.

"Naw, I'm not into that either, Valarie. I mean, every so often some guy suggests it. But let me tell you about the guys who watch those movies in porno shops. Those guys are real weirdos. I mean, they even start hugging and caressing the machine that's showing the movies! That kind of guy can get dangerous, real dangerous. I don't want them coming in here."

Harvey apparently didn't know that I knew about the videotapes he was making. Should I blurt out that I knew about them? Maybe I'd better be coy. I sure didn't want him to yell for Angelo! And I didn't want to get Candi in trouble for telling me.

"No, that's not what I mean, Harvey," I said. "I mean, maybe you could hire somebody to come and take movies of us working, and you could sell those movies to the porno shops. I bet you could make a mint doing that."

Harvey's face reddened, and I knew I had him now.

"If anybody tried to bring a hidden camera into my place," he thundered, "so help me, I'd kill him!"

"I know what you mean, Harvey. I mean, if somebody tried to take movies of me and some guy without my permission, I'd really get ticked off. In fact, I'd probably call Angelo on him."

Harvey shifted uneasily in his chair. "What are you getting at, Valarie?" he demanded. "What are you trying to say?"

"Harvey, I know about that video camera looking into my room. You've been making tapes of me and the guys, haven't you?"

"Who told you about that?"

I wasn't about to put the finger on Candi. She'd been helpful to me so far. And she could make life pretty miserable for me if she wanted to.

"Come on, Harvey," I said. "Do I look stupid? You're using the oldest trick in the book. I've been around. I know what the girls on the streets say about these massage parlors. In fact, I know of one on Forty-fourth Street that has a big one-way glass. They have one group of guys in there with the girl, and another group outside looking through the mirror. The weird part is that the customers on the outside pay more than the customers on the inside! It's really weird."

"Are you kidding?" Harvey asked. "I never heard of that."

I hadn't either. But I knew New York City is a big place, and there had to be things Harvey would have no way of knowing about. How could he prove I was lying?

"So as soon as I saw all those black dots, and when you got so huffy about my asking about them," I went on, "I figured what was up. So when I got a chance, I went over and checked out the wall. Sure enough, I found that glass one and could see the lens on the other side of it. I figured it was a video camera—that would be the easiest to operate. Well, I almost covered the lens over with my stockings, but I figured that would make you mad. Then I decided it really wouldn't hurt anything. After all, Harvey, you've been nice to me. You bailed me out. You gave me a bag of dope. You gave me a job and a warm room to stay in. So I guess I couldn't be mad at you for something like that, could I?"

All the color had drained from Harvey's face by now. I knew he was wondering which direction I was going with this!

"Well, maybe I should have told you yesterday," he finally said. "But I was worried that it might make you nervous and self-conscious, and that would drive away my customers. I don't really like to do this kind of thing, but you know how it is. This is a tricky business. You've got to make the money while you can. And videotapes are one of the hottest items on the market today. All I'm trying to do is put a little money ahead for retirement. In this business, you never know how long you'll be around."

"No problem, Harvey. I just wish you'd told me. Man, I bet you're making a bundle on those tapes, aren't you?"

"Yeah, I do okay on them," he responded. "Tell you what. I'll give you an extra fifty dollars a night for the tapes. Okay?"

I hated the idea of someone making movies of me and some guy—and I hated even more the idea of those perverts watching. But what could I do? I was trapped in the Blue Lagoon. So I'd better try to make the best of a bad situation.

"Okay, if you make it a hundred," I blurted out.

"No problem, kid," Harvey responded. He pulled out a wad of hundreds, whipped one off, and shoved it at me.

"Here's for last night," he said. "And no hard feelings?"

"No hard feelings."

He came around and put his arms around me. "Valarie, you and I are going to make a great team!" he said, beaming.

I wasn't all that happy about it. But a hundred bucks was a hundred bucks. In fact, it translated into four bags of dope. And that was a language that a junkie like me understood.

I stuffed the bill into my jeans and walked to my room to get things ready for my first customer. I felt a little depressed as I looked at that black dot that hid the lens of the TV camera. Harvey was right. I did feel a little self-conscious about it now. But then I thought about the hundred bucks a night. Maybe I could rationalize that I was a great model who was geting paid to perform in front of a camera. Maybe I'd get used to it. But right now it really embarrassed me.

Next I walked to the reception lounge where I waited. A little later when my first customer came in, I gave him a massage and the extra he wanted. He gave me seventy-five dollars.

I quickly got two more. Then at about nine a well-dressed man came in. I was alone in the reception lounge. He asked for Martha.

"She's busy," I said. "How about me?"

"Martha's my favorite," he responded. "She knows exactly what I need."

I looked him over closely. Was this the pusher? He certainly looked like a businessman. But wait. he didn't have any briefcase. Candi said the pusher carried the dope in a briefcase. Besides, this guy looked like he was good for at least two hundred dollars. I'd make a play for him.

"You know who I am?" I asked.

He looked me up and down. "Nope," he responded. "I've never seen you before that I know of."

"Well, that's because I just got in from Los Angeles. I've been working out there the past two years. I'm known as one of the best in the business. I came out here to New York because I heard the customers are gentle and kind and pay you what you're worth. And, mister, I'm really worth a lot!"

He chuckled at my directness.

"Why don't you try me?" I suggested. "Just once?"

"Well, okay," he said reluctantly. "But I want to warn you that I'm not your ordinary type. My demands are a little different."

That didn't throw me. I'd discovered that all the guys who came in thought they were different. But basically they were all after the same thing. But I'd learned to play along to make them feel important. I'd learned that hustling on the streets.

"Mister, I can tell you're different," I said. "I mean you look like a man that any girl would want—and to think that today is my lucky day!"

I threw my arms around him and felt him begin to respond. This was going to be an easy two hundred bucks!

I led him back to my room. As soon as he got inside, he started pulling off his shirt. He'd been through this before, so maybe it wouldn't take too long.

"Okay, lay down on my massage bench and watch my technique," I told him, pointing to the bench.

He started to mumble something. Then I noticed small beads of sweat breaking out on his forehead. He seemed awfully nervous. Didn't he trust me?

Trying to reassure him, I said, "Hey, listen, there is no

one like me. You've got the best this time. Now trust me."

When he pulled out a handkerchief to wipe the sweat from his forehead, I saw his hand trembling.

"What's the matter?" I asked gently. "You afraid?"

He put the handkerchief back into his pocket and started trembling all over. Was this character a pervert?

"Come on, don't be afraid," I soothed. "In just a few minutes you're going to feel absolutely great!"

I noticed that his eyes didn't rove up and down my body the way the other guys' did. Something was bothering him.

"Listen, you're really tense, aren't you?" I asked. "You've probably had a rough day. Mister, I can relax you so that you'll think you're in heaven!"

He finally got onto the massage bench, and I went to work. As I began to stroke his face, I could feel him relax.

I was working my way down his back when he suddenly turned over, looked straight into my eyes, and asked, "Will you marry me?"

It wasn't the first time I had run into this question. Every so often there was some guy who felt it was his destiny in life to snatch you out of the horrible pit you had gotten yourself into. I guess these guys saw themselves as knights in shining armor. The idea of marriage was okay, but these guys really had pretty tarnished armor, and I'm sure they wouldn't have made good husbands.

I acted as though I hadn't heard what he said and kept on working, so he pushed my hands away and said, "Will you marry me?"

I laughed. "No, I'm not the marrying type," I replied. "Besides, I don't think I could ever settle down."

He raised up, grabbed my shoulders, and gripped tightly. "I'm going to marry you!" he announced with finality.

I looked into his eyes and realized he was dead serious!

So I gently took his hands and tried to move them away. Instead I felt him grip tighter. And when I started to step back, he dug his fingernails into my armpits. Now what was I going to do?

"Hey, mister, don't try anything funny," I warned. "This isn't a chapel where you can get married on the spur of the moment. I want to check out the guy I marry. What kind of a husband would you be anyway?"

"I'd be the best kind," he responded immediately. "I would be a great husband. I mean, if you need me. And you really do need me!"

Why hadn't I let this nut wait for Martha? Why did I have to be so greedy? Maybe if I humored him. . . .

So I said, "Mister, I'm the kind of girl who likes to party all day and all night. I can go for seven days and seven nights of partying and not get tired. You sure you want that kind of a wife?"

"Marry me, please marry me!" he begged.

Since humor wasn't getting the job done, I tried the scare tactic. "Mister, if you don't get your hands off of me this instant," I threatened, "I'm going to call the bouncer. He'll make mincemeat out of you. Now let me go."

Once again I tried pushing him away, but he wasn't about to budge. Should I scream for Angelo? I hated to do that since this character was supposed to be a regular. Was he putting me on about that? But how could he know to ask for Martha if he weren't?

Next I tried a smile—maybe that would disarm him. Yet he seemed to get more tense. Finally, I felt him relax and let go. Believe me, I relaxed, too!

"Okay, that's it," he announced. "The massage is over."

I sure wasn't about to suggest anything else. I wanted to get this nut out of my room just as soon as possible.

He hopped off the table and started to put his shirt on. But as he buttoned it, he stared at me strangely. Somehow I felt he had something else in mind.

I edged toward the door, but he yelled, "Stop right there! I'm not through yet!"

No way was I going to do anything else with this nut, so I yelled back, "Mister, as far as I'm concerned, your massage is over!"

He leaped—but not at me. He merely yanked his coat off the rack. Relieved, I stood my ground.

Instead of putting his coat on, he thrust his hand into a pocket and jerked it out quickly. Then I heard the snap. He stood there, feet apart, his switchblade pointing menacingly at my heart!

I gasped, and he said, "Now are you going to agree to marry me?"

This guy was a bigger nut than I realized!

"Hey, mister," I replied nervously, "like I told you, I'm not the marrying kind. And I'm sure not about to marry somebody who just comes in off the street. I don't even know your name!"

He was within two steps of me, and I froze where I was. If he took one more step, I was yelling—regular customer or not!

When he took that step, I screamed, "Angelo! Angelo! Angelo!"

The door flew open, but instead of Angelo, there stood Martha!

"Michael Galvanek, you put that knife down!" she screamed.

Startled by Martha's sudden appearance, he looked toward her as menacingly as he had looked toward me. Was he going to kill us both?

"Get out while you can, Martha!" I yelled. "Get Angelo! This guy looks like he's ready to kill!"

"Didn't you hear what I said, Mr. Galvanek?" Martha said sternly. "You put that knife down, and we'll talk about getting married next week."

Married? What on earth was going on around here? Was he really a regular, and had Martha accepted his proposal of marriage? She must really want to get out of this place to marry a kook like this character! And I'd be delighted for her to take him somewhere and talk to him so I could escape with my life!

Mr. Galvanek frowned at Martha, unmoved by her command. Then he turned his attention back to me.

"Okay, Mr. Galvanek, have it your way," Martha yelled again. "But no more talk about marriage."

My heart was beating like crazy. One more step and he would be close enough to plunge that knife into my chest. And the crazy look in his eyes told me he wouldn't hesitate to do it!

When Martha turned to leave, he seemed to sense that things weren't working out as he had planned. Slowly he lowered his arm. Martha stepped next to him, gently removed the switchblade from his hand, took his arm, and said softly, "Now, Mr. Galvanek, you come with me. I was hoping you'd come today. We have to make more plans for our marriage. Which church was it you said you wanted to get married in?"

Chatting amiably about details like that, she led him out the door. He glanced back at me and smiled sheepishly. I heaved a huge sigh of relief. I owed my life to Martha!

I heard a door slam down the hall and figured she must have taken him to her room. But why? Wouldn't she have done better to have taken him outside?

Well, at least he wasn't here! Feeling faint, I went over and collapsed onto my massage bench. That was too close!

I sat there staring at the floor, hardly daring to believe what I had just been through. I could have been lying on that floor with my guts slashed out or with a knife through my heart!

I must have sat there for an hour, too scared to move. And when someone knocked on my door, I jumped straight up. "Who's there?" I asked nervously

The door opened, and there stood Martha again. "That ought to teach you a lesson," she said piously.

"What do you mean, teach me a lesson? I owe you a big thank you for saving my life."

"Yeah, you really do," she responded coldly. "But that's not why I came back. I came because I heard that Mr. Galvanek asked for me, and you talked him into taking you. That really ticks me off, Valarie."

That's all she was mad about? As far as I was concerned, she could have the nut forever!

"I'm sorry," I said lamely. "I guess it was a misunderstanding. I thought we were supposed to try to keep the customers from going out after they come in. You were busy, and I—"

"Listen, Valarie," she interrupted angrily. "You've got to understand the rules of the game. My customers are mine. You start pushing into my territory, and you're going to be in big trouble. I don't care who the guy is. If he asks for me, you keep your claws off of him. Or the next time you may not come out of it alive. You read me?"

"Listen, Martha, I'll never take another of your customers. I learned my lesson."

"Okay. But remember, you were lucky this time. You were lucky I just happened to be going by your door when you yelled for Angelo. The big oaf was in the rest room, and it would have been a while before he ever got to you. So don't you ever try anything like that again! Do you hear me?"

I was willing to admit I was wrong, but I sure didn't like Martha's arrogant attitude. I was almost ready to reach out and slap her silly. But I had to admit she had saved my life.

So instead of arguing the point, I asked, "What's with this Mr. Galvanek? He asked me to marry him and got all upset when I wouldn't agree to it. I've had tricks try that line on me before, but I usually figured it was because they felt guilty over what they were doing."

"He really doesn't want to marry you, Valarie," Martha responded, laughing. "He's a nut. But you've got to humor nuts. He pays good for his massages, so I humor him, and he keeps coming back. All he really wants is a massage."

"That wasn't all he wanted from me," I told her. "He grabbed me and wanted me to say right then that I would marry him. I knew he was a nut, but—"

"You'd better believe he's a nut," she interrupted. "I remember the first time he came in here. He got his massage, and then he announced he wanted to marry me."

"So what did you say?"

"Well, when you get a nut, my rule is: Be nutty yourself." She laughed, but I didn't see anything funny about the situation. I was still shaking from that close encounter with death.

"When he asked me to marry him, I said sure," Martha went on. "I even began to brag about what a handsome man he was and what a great husband he would be. That got him calmed down, and I told him to come back the next week for another massage—then we could discuss our plans for marriage."

"You really said you'd marry that nut?"

Martha nodded. "Sure. Why not? He came back the next week and got his massage. Then we started talking about marriage."

"You've got to be kidding!" I exploded.

Martha laughed as she said, "Come on, Valarie, don't be stupid. No way would I marry a freak like Mr. Galvanek. But we've been planning our 'marriage' for over a year now. He comes back once a week. In fact, several times, we've even set dates. But when the date gets close, he always finds some excuse for postponing the wedding. I don't have to worry about him. He's afraid to get married. But he's got this crazy fantasy about me, and—"

"If he fantasizes about you, why did he want to marry me?" I interrupted.

"Valarie, he doesn't care who he fantasizes about," Martha replied. "You, me, Candi—any girl who will massage him the rest of his life. I don't really think it's the person at all. He just feels a special closeness to any girl who massages him, and he starts talking about marriage."

"Martha, I'm sure that nut would have killed me if you hadn't come in," I said, still shaking as I thought back about it. "Don't you worry that he might kill you sometime? Seems to me you are sure taking a big chance with him."

"Oh, come off it," she replied. "I can handle nuts. Like I said, be nutty with nuts. Besides, I make good money off him. I even got him to pay me for your massage."

I started to grab the money she held in her hand, but I realized I did owe her something for what she had done for me. So I merely said, "Well, if I get any more nuts like Mr. Galvanek, I'm sending them down to you."

"It's not that easy, Valarie. Sometimes an ordinary guy

comes walking in. You'd swear he was a common, okay Joe. But before you know what's happening, he's pulled a knife or a gun on you. You can't tell the crazies from the ordinary people by the way they look. So keep your eyes open and your guard up!"

"How?" I asked.

"As soon as a guy pulls off his jacket, you grab it. Fold it in half and quickly run your hand along it searching for knives or guns."

"But what happens if I find one?"

"Just tilt the jacket so the weapon falls to the floor. When the guy realizes you know he has a knife or a gun, he won't use it. You see, guns and knives are for surprises."

I nodded. That made sense.

"But don't stuff the weapon back in his jacket," she cautioned. "That gives him the possibility of surprise again. Leave it on the table where you can see it. I tell you, that will work."

Martha was pretty smart in handling these crazies. I guess she had had to learn from experience, but it seemed to me these lessons were terribly dangerous. I hoped I didn't have to learn them the hard way. But I'd sure never forget what she had just told me. From now on, I'd check all jackets for guns or knives!

I was still nervously pacing back and forth in my room when Martha suggested I'd better get back out front. "You haven't been out there since I took Mr. Galvanek out of here, have you?" she asked.

I nodded.

"Well, you'd better get out there," she warned. "If Harvey finds out you're goofing off back here, he'll beat you to a bloody pulp. He gets ticked off when we're not working. And with Harvey, being frightened is no excuse!"

When I started down the hallway, Harvey yelled from behind me, "Valarie, you get into my office right now!"

I didn't like the way he said that. Was I about to get a going over? Or had that Martha ratted to him that I had tried to steal one of her customers?

7

With a great deal of trepidation I entered Harvey's office. "Sit down!" he roared.

I sat on the edge of the chair, ready to run if I needed to.

"What's the matter?" I asked.

"Nothing really," he replied, fidgeting with a pencil. "It's just that business has slumped since the weather turned colder. I'm going to have to try something new."

"Such as?"

"Valarie, I want you to stand out in the street, look alluring, and invite men inside."

"What?" I yelled. "You want the cops on me? They'll arrest me for solicitation if I'm out on the street like a hooker!"

"Valarie, like I told you, I run a legitimate business here. I'll take care of those little details you mentioned. I just want you out there drumming up a little more business. My expenses have gone way up, and I'll have to shut this place down if things don't improve."

"What's in it for me?" I asked.

He jumped up, pointed his finger at me, and snapped, "Don't get smart with me! Just a snap of my fingers, and you're back in the slammer. Did you forget that Big Daddy got you out of jail—or that he can send you back?"

Come to think of it, I had forgotten. Harvey had me over a barrel, and we both knew it.

"So you want me out in the street inviting men in. Right?"

"That's all."

"What about the other girls?"

"They'll be out there too," he answered, "but only one girl at a time. When you get a guy and bring him in, then I'll send one of the other girls out, so there'll be one of you out there all the time."

"What if one of our regulars comes?"

"Nothing's changed on that. That'll mean you can stay in out of the cold a little longer!" Harvey snickered.

I was beginning to see some value in having regulars now! I sure didn't look forward to having to stand out in the cold.

"When does this start?" I asked.

"Right now. Get on out there."

Reluctantly I headed for the street and started smiling at passing men, just as I had done when I was out on the streets on my own. When one guy looked interested, I said, "Hey, mister, want a relaxing massage to warm you up?"

"Sure, why not?" he responded and took my arm.

I led him inside to my room where we went through the massage and everything else. He paid me fifty bucks—not too bad.

I went back on the street, and it wasn't too long before I got another one. Maybe Harvey was right. Maybe this was a good way to improve business.

Several nights later when I was on the street, I noticed a woman and a young lady walking toward me, sort of looking me over. I tried to ignore them by staring in the opposite direction. But when they stopped right in front of me, I wondered what in the world they were up to. "Do you work in this massage parlor?" the woman asked.

I turned away, but she repeated, "You work here?"

"Hey, lady, move on down the block, will you?" I answered coldly. "I'm busy."

"Well, I don't want to take any of your time or be a bother to you," she went on apologetically. "I just thought maybe you needed help."

I stared at the two for the first time and tried to size them up. There was something unusual about them. Were they undercover cops? What were they up to?

"Ma'am, why don't you just state your business and then move on down the street?" I said.

She pushed a brown brochure toward me and said, "I'm Mom Benton from the Walter Hoving Home. This," she pointed to the young lady, "is Jennifer. She's a graduate of our program. We are out here on the streets, talking to girls who have problems with drug addiction."

I glanced at the brochure and announced. "That's nice. But I don't need any drug rehabilitation program."

"I know you don't need a drug rehabilitation program," the woman responded. "What you need is Jesus Christ."

I stepped back. So that was it—two religious nuts!

Mom Benton must have noticed my reaction, for she laughed as she said, "Now don't let that bother you. You may not understand it, but the greatest thing that could ever happen to you would be to receive Jesus Christ as your Saviour. He'd set you free from this filthy place you have to work in and would deliver you from your drug habit."

How did she know I worked in a "filthy place"?

"Ma'am, have you ever been in a massage parlor?"

"No, but my husband has been down here with the vice squad."

So they were tied in with the cops!

"Your old man a cop?" I asked her.

"No, he directs the Walter Hoving Home," she replied. "But he also writes books. He was doing some research for a book called *Patti*. The vice squad took him through some massage parlors so he could see what they were like. He said they are rather filthy inside. He also said you get more than a massage when you're a customer there. You know what I mean?"

Of course I knew what she meant, but I wasn't about to admit anything. If these people were on speaking terms with the vice squad, I wanted to be pretty careful what I said. But I still couldn't help but like the woman. She kept smiling—one of the most pleasant smiles I had ever seen.

But talking to her wasn't helping me with what I was supposed to be out here doing. No guys would stop when I was talking to these two. Somehow I had to get her to move along.

"Well I'm no junkie, and I'm no prostitute," I told her. "My dad owns this massage parlor, and we run a legitimate business. Anyone can come in for a massage, and that's all we do."

Jennifer laughed softly. "Well, isn't that a coincidence?" she remarked. "I used to use almost the same line myself. Only I said it was my uncle who ran the massage parlor."

"You worked in a massage parlor?" I asked.

"Yeah," she replied. "Four years ago I worked at one on Eighth Avenue between Forty-third and Forty-fourth."

"Your uncle owned one in that area?"

"No, you know who owns these places—the mob. And the massage-parlor bit was just a front for a house of prostitution."

I had mixed feelings about these two. Some things about them bothered me, but I still found myself almost drawn to them. They were sure different!

"You're putting me on, man," I told Jennifer. "No way will I believe you ever worked in a massage parlor."

She pulled off her coat, pulled up her sleeve, and pointed. "You recognize these?" she asked.

I nodded. "That's your track."

"You'd better believe that's my track," she replied. "I was hooked on the stuff for eight years. You name it, and I've done it—massage parlors, prostitute on Forty-second Street, junkie. I was even a dope carrier!"

She might be telling me lies about the rest of it, but that track told me she was telling the truth about one thing. I had a track too—but I'd never tell her that.

"Okay, so you were in the game," I said reluctantly. "But it's true that my dad and I have this legitimate business here. All we do is give massages."

Jennifer had her coat back on by this time. Suddenly she pointed her finger right into my face and said, "I don't know who you are, but I am sure the Lord let me make contact with you tonight."

Her finger pointing at me like that made me uncomfortable, and I tried to back away. But she stepped right up to me and went on: "You may not realize this, but God brought Mom B and me into contact with you for a purpose. I believe we're here tonight just for you. And the message we have for you is one of love and hope. First, God loves you. His Son, Jesus, loved you so much that He died for all your sins. The second thing is that Mom B and I really love you, too. We want you to come up to our home and find love like you've never experienced before."

I knew I ought to run back into the safety of the massage

parlor. These people were getting entirely too personal. But something, almost like a magnetic force, seemed to be drawing me to them. One part of me wanted to hear more. Another part of me wanted to tell them to get lost.

"God has given us a beautiful home up in Garrison, New York," Mom B said. "There, many girls just like you have been set free from the curse of drug addiction—girls like Jennifer here."

"Excuse me," Jennifer said, "I guess we got to talking and really didn't introduce ourselves properly. "I'm Jennifer Rauscher, and this is Mrs. Benton. We all call her Mom B. What's your name?"

"Valarie Lambert," I responded, overcoming the temptation to give them a fictitious name.

"Valarie, I know you are out here working," Jennifer said, "and I know you've got to get on with it. But if you can just take a moment, I think I can tell you a little bit about me."

"Okay," I said, "but for just a moment." I knew that Harvey or Angelo would be out if I didn't bring in a customer soon.

"I had a terrible upbringing," she started. "My father was an alcoholic, and I never remember a day when my mother was sober. When I was twelve, the Welfare Department said my parents weren't fit, and they put me in a foster home. That's when my world fell apart."

I felt my throat tighten. I sure remembered some of the things I'd been through, too.

"When I was in that foster home," Jennifer continued, "something inside of me blew apart. I ran away. Even though I was living in Indiana, I ended up here in New York City—down at the bus depot at the Port Authority."

I nodded. It seemed as though all the runaways ended up there.

"I'd no sooner got off the bus than some slick guy picked me up. I bet you know what he was, don't you?"

"A pimp?"

She nodded. "But I was lucky. About a week after I was out on the streets working for that pimp, the cops picked me up and sent me back to Indiana. My trip to New York scared me to death, and I said I would never get involved in something like this again. But when I went back to school, I kept on drinking, started smoking pot, and the next thing I knew I had packed my bags and ended up here again."

"Same deal?" I asked.

"No, this time I decided to do it on my own. I picked up a trick, and that was the beginning of a life of prostitution, drugs, you name it. My habit got so bad that I had to have drugs just to get straight. I've been in and out of jail so many times I've lost count. I've taken overdoses, some of them deliberately. But, thank God, I lived. Some of my friends didn't. I was in a hell on earth."

I knew where this girl was coming from. She knew the life.

"Then one evening I was out on Forty-second and Eighth and ran into Mom B and her husband. We call him Brother B. They started talking to me about Jesus and how He offered me hope, a way out of the mess I was trapped in. Right there on the street, amid all the hell of that area, I gave my heart to Jesus. My world turned completely around."

Her story was so unbelievable that I was staring right into her face. That's when I noticed the tears forming in her eyes.

"It was the most beautiful thing that ever happened to me," she went on. "I didn't think there was any hope. I just knew that someday I'd die of an overdose or a pimp would kill me or some pervert would cut out my guts. But when I gave my heart to Jesus you wouldn't believe the peace I received!

"I went with the Bentons up to the Walter Hoving Home, where I learned to live according to the teachings of the Bible. That was four years ago, Valarie. I haven't touched drugs since. That's why I can tell you it works! I know. And God has placed on my heart a burden to share this good news with others."

"Valarie, you do need to be set free," Mom B added. "There is hope for you."

The lump in my throat almost choked me. Then the tears started. The next thing I knew I felt Mom B's loving arms hugging me. It felt so good!

"Valarie, there are a lot of people like you who are existing in a life of sin and who think there's no hope," she said softly. "I know you don't know Jennifer or me at all. But if you'll trust us, why don't you come up to our home with us? I believe God let us meet tonight so that you could give your life to Jesus. How about it?"

Something within me urged me to do what they asked. But could I really go with them right now? Just like that? I was scared!

Before I could respond, however, I felt Mom B suddenly let go of me. Someone roughly grabbed my shoulder and jerked me around. I looked straight into Harvey's angry face. Cursing loudly, he shouted, "I didn't send you out here for a sideshow. Now you come with me!"

I tried to pull away, but he only gripped tighter.

"Please, sir, Valarie needs help!" Mom B implored.

He didn't respond. He simply jerked me inside and slammed the door. Then he started in. "I was watching you out there!" he yelled. "You can't afford to spend all that time talking to those stupid tourists. When they come around, just tell them to get lost or you'll pull your switchblade. That'll send them on their way."

"But they weren't tourists," I protested weakly. "They're from a home where they help girls."

"What do you mean, 'help girls'? The only help you need is from me, Valarie, and don't you forget it! I'm the one who got you out of jail, and I'm the one who can put you right back in there if you step out of line. Do you understand that?"

I nodded, knowing I didn't dare challenge Harvey. But as I brushed the tears from my eyes, I knew what I was thinking. Harvey was wrong. I needed a kind of help he couldn't possibly give me. Something deep within me cried out that Mom B and Jennifer had found something real—something I needed. Where did they say that place was? Maybe I could contact them when I got away from this place.

It was then I realized I had dropped the brochure they had given me. Maybe if I went out right away, I could find it.

"You want me to go back out?" I asked Harvey.

He peered outside. "Not yet," he responded. "Those two characters are still out there. I've got to get rid of them. They'll drive away all my business."

I could hear Harvey yelling at them outside, but I couldn't tell what he was saying. Apparently those two didn't move easily, for he must have been out there at least ten minutes!

When he finally came in, he looked exhausted. "Those are two of the most persistent women I've ever encountered!" he said. "I told them to get out of here, or I'd call the cops. That didn't even faze them. The girl argued with me, but I guess they finally gave up. I waited to be sure they were long gone. So now get out on that street, Valarie, and get a customer—or I'll really give you something to think about!"

As I went out the door, I looked in both directions, hoping against hope to catch a glimpse of them. Nothing. Well, if I ever saw them again, I'd sure seriously consider going with them. Anything would be better than life in this hellhole.

I even searched the area trying to find the brochure I had dropped. There was plenty of other trash blowing in the wind, but nowhere could I locate that brown brochure. Maybe the whole thing just wasn't meant for me after all.

We kept working the streets for another month or so. I met another of Martha's regulars out there—without realizing he was hers. She really got her nose out of joint and told me in no uncertain terms that Dr. Vines belonged to her. When he paid me four hundred dollars, you can believe I wanted to keep him. So I said, "Next time he comes, we'll let him decide whose massage he likes best."

She mumbled something, and I knew that once again our relationship was strained to the breaking point. My big worry was that she'd quit selling me drugs. Maybe I ought to start looking for another connection.

I was out on the street again when a guy walked up and looked me over. I asked if he wanted a massage, and he replied easily, "That's what I came for!"

I laughed at his directness, but something about him just wasn't right. Still I knew I had to take the chance. Harvey kept leaning on us to deliver more customers and even threatened to up his part of the take.

So I brought the guy to my room. And was I in for a big surprise!

8

I didn't say much as I massaged the little guy's back. But I was sure wondering what there was about him that made me so uneasy. Was he perverted? What kind of torture would he expect me to administer? The fleeting thought that he might be a cop crossed my mind, but I dismissed it quickly. He was too small to be a cop. I remembered reading somewhere the physical specifications they had for cops, and this guy sure didn't look as though he'd qualify.

When I got through with the massage and asked if there was anything else he'd like, he said no. He asked how much he owed me, and I told him twenty-five dollars. After all, I wanted to make something on the deal!

He paid without comment, put his shirt back on, and then said, "Want to buy some drugs?"

So that was it! I knew the guy was different, but I hadn't thought about his being a pusher. Of course, I didn't know him or his angle, so I played it cool.

"Drugs?" I asked in surprise. "Man, I don't need drugs. I'm scared to death of needles."

The guy laughed. "You think I'm a dumb nut?" he asked. "I saw the tracks on your arm. They're fresh."

There was no way I could hide those tracks.

"Oh, those," I said lamely. "Yeah, I used to take drugs,

but, man, I don't do that anymore. Man, I'm clean now."

He chuckled as he said, "You really must think I'm stupid. I know a junkie when I see a junkie—and you're a junkie. Like I said, you've got fresh tracks. You've been getting off every day, haven't you?"

The guy knew the business. There was no sense lying to him. "Okay, okay," I admitted, "but I didn't know if you might be an undercover cop. You can't be too careful in this business."

He laughed again. "Me, a cop? They wouldn't take me, kid, unless I grew three more inches and added thirty-five pounds. But I know what you mean. That's why I don't just walk into a massage parlor and ask a girl if she wants to buy drugs. I check her out first. I like the way you handle yourself. You've got dignity and class."

If anybody complimented me on my dignity, I would be his friend forever. That was one thing I desperately wanted to have—and felt I had so little of in this business. So even though the guy was scrawny, I was beginning to warm up to him.

"How much a bag?" I asked.

"Twenty bucks."

"Not bad. I've been paying twenty-five. How come you're cheaper? You've got good stuff?"

"I've got the best—from Turkey! But I can charge less because I pick my customers carefully. If somebody I don't know walks up to me on the street, I get at least twenty-five dollars, sometimes more. But for my regular customers, it's only twenty dollars."

"Okay, I'll take four bags," I said. "You wait here. I've got to go upstairs and get my own money."

"Uh, I've got a little problem," the guy responded. "You see, I only brought one bag with me. I don't want to get caught with four bags on me in case I get busted. You know what I mean?"

This guy was really smart.

"Why don't you just give me twenty bucks from that twenty-five I just paid you? Then I can be on my way. I'll bring the other three bags back later. Okay?"

"No, I can't do that," I said reluctantly. "The guy I work for would throw me out in the street if he thought I was using his money to buy drugs. I have to go get my own money. It'll be just a minute, that's all."

"Well, okay, but don't you dare tell anyone what you're doing or who I am."

"Are you kidding? Man, if I can save five bucks a bag, I'm not telling a soul!"

Just as I started up the steps, Candi called, "Hey, Valarie, wait up a minute."

I stopped and turned. What did she want?

"Who's the guy in your room?"

Candi must have spotted that pusher. Junkies can almost smell one! Well, he told me not to tell, so I played dumb.

"He's a distant cousin of mine," I lied. "He lives in Jersey. His name is Gary Falk."

I started up the stairs, but she pulled me around and asked, "You sure you know him?"

"Sure. Wouldn't I know my own cousin?"

"Valarie, I saw you go down the hall with that guy, and I've been talking to Martha about him. There's something strange about him. You'd better watch it."

"I can take care of myself, Candi. You take care of your customers, and I'll take care of mine. Okay?"

She grabbed my arm, but I jerked away, yelling, "You keep your hands off of me!"

"Valarie, for crying out loud, I just came down here to

warn you. I didn't come down to pick a fight. I just wanted
to tell you that I got this feeling there's something wrong
with that guy. Did he have an iron on him?"

"An iron? What are you talking about?"

"You're really stupid. Did he have a gun?"

"A gun? My cousin doesn't carry a gun. Why should he
have a gun?"

"I guess I'm going to have to sit down and educate you
some more, Valarie. Every once in a while detectives from
the vice squad come in here. Some of them even ask for a
massage. But you can tell them by their guns. All those
guys carry guns. Did this guy have a gun?"

"Of course not. I mean, I didn't see one."

"Sometimes they carry a shoulder holster. Did you
watch him take his clothes off?"

"Sure. There was no gun."

"Yeah, but that's only one place. Detectives also keep
guns on their legs. Did you check his legs?"

"Check his legs? Why would I check his legs? I was massaging his back."

"Listen, Valarie, I'll bet that guy has a gun on his leg.
You should have felt his legs. You know, just kind of
lightly touch him. You've got to check these guys out."

I couldn't tell Candi he was a pusher, so I said, "Okay, if
it'll make you breathe easier, I'll go back and rub my hands
up and down his legs. Then I'll let you know."

"Valarie, if that guy's a detective, you'd better watch him
closely. I mean, you really have to be careful. He may even
plant dope on you so he can bust you for possession. These
guys from the vice squad really delight in busting girls from
massage parlors. I think they get a medal from the police
commissioner, or something like that. So watch him
closely."

Thanking Candi for her concern, I ran upstairs and got a

twenty, then ran back down to my massage room. I knew I had to find out whether or not the guy was on the level.

He was standing there waiting for me, and when he saw me, he extended the bag of dope. I started to reach for it, but something told me this was too easy.

"Sorry to be gone so long," I told him, "but I just ran into a little problem. You see, I met my boss down the hall, and he said he hadn't seen you here before. So he told me to come back here and give you the best back rub you'd ever had. He wanted to be sure you came back."

"You mean I'm going to get two rubs for my twenty-five bucks?"

"You got it, mister. It's our two-for-one special today! You don't mind, do you? You've got the time?"

"Have I got the time? Baby, if I get a free rub, I've got all the time in the world!"

My plan was working. I didn't think he'd fall for it so easily.

When he took off his shirt and undershirt, I watched closely. Certainly he wasn't carrying a gun. Then he stretched out on the massage table. "Now I've got to give you a really super-duper rub," I said. "Let me get up on your back."

I jumped up on the table, laid my body over his, and began to rub my hands seductively over his back and sides.

"Hey, how come you didn't give me this kind of rub the first time?" he asked. "This is great!"

"I'm giving you the full treatment!" I said.

I started rubbing his legs, but when I got down around his ankles, the guy jerked. But I felt something hard on his ankle, and I jumped off the table.

Candi was right. This guy had a gun strapped to his leg!

The disappointment on his face really clouded his features as he asked, "Hey, how come you quit so fast? Is that it?"

"Yeah, that's it. I don't want to overdo it. I've got to leave you wanting more so that you'll come back again."

"You'd better believe I'm coming back again!" he responded. "Like maybe tomorrow?"

"Sure, why not? I'm here every day!"

The guy slid off the table without saying another word about the dope. I knew I'd better not buy it now. But what was I going to tell him when he asked?

He bent over, as if he were tying his shoelaces. When he stood up, I found myself looking down the barrel of his pistol!

I bolted for the door, but he caught me with his other hand and told me, "Lady, I don't know who you are or what your game is, but I know exactly why you gave me that second back rub. It was to check me out to see if I carried an iron, wasn't it?"

"Mister, I don't know what you're talking about," I said as coolly as I could under the circumstances. "My boss told me to treat every customer with respect. You're a customer, and I'm a massager. Now whether you carry a gun or not is up to you. I just did what my boss told me. I gave you a free back rub."

"Well, let me tell you something," he replied, lowering the gun a little. "When you're a drug dealer, you learn to be smart. I don't know how much you know about the drug business, but there are some pretty simple facts about it. One is that drug dealers will sometimes try to rip off other dealers. You know how it is about dope. There are no rules to this game. So I carry an iron for protection. I'm small, and people think they can take advantage of me. But this rod gives me power. I mean, big power, baby."

I was still trying to figure out if the guy was on the level. He still could be a cop.

"Listen, I know what you're thinking," he went on. "You figure I'm a cop 'cause I carry a gun. Well, let me put your mind at ease. I'm not a cop. Besides, how do I know you're not an undercover agent planted by the vice squad down here to catch drug dealers like me? You know, cops plant women in places like this. You knew that, didn't you?"

"No, I sure didn't know that," I replied in surprise.

"Well, they do," he went on. "I knew one up on Forty-third Street. Fortunately one of my customers who went there tipped me off about her. She gave a good massage, but I sure didn't offer her any drugs!"

"But why would cops do something like that?"

"Listen, you know why? Most of these massage parlors are controlled by the mob. I mean, there's big money in these places. And you know these are just fronts for prostitution. I know if I had wanted to, we could have gone beyond the back rub, couldn't we?"

I was kind of embarrassed by his directness. If this guy was a drug dealer, he sure knew his way around. But was he a cop?

"I'm going to tell you something else," he said. "There's a girl here in the Blue Lagoon named Martha who sells drugs. Maybe you've been getting your drugs from her. She buys them from Robert Sandelman, and he buys them from Charlie Spector."

This guy was sounding less and less like a cop. He knew his way around in the drug world too well.

"Okay, but you can't blame me for being careful, can you?"

He laughed easily. "Of course not. Like I say, I just knew you had the touch. It's a good thing you checked me out because now I know you're not an undercover cop."

"Well, to tell you the truth, one of the girls here named Candi was the one who was suspicious of you," I said.

"Candi? Sure, I should have suspected her," he said. "She's a junkie too, isn't she?"

"I don't like that term."

"Okay, have it your way. But Candi's on drugs. Right?"

"Yeah. We both buy from Martha. It's safer than going out on the street, you know."

"Maybe not," the guy responded. "Maybe you've been lucky so far. But let me tell you something about that Charlie Spector—the one Sandelman gets the drugs from that he brings to Martha. That Charlie is one of the most vicious, dirtiest pushers around. You've really got to watch that guy. Sometimes he sells just milk sugar quinine—no stuff at all in it. Sometimes he laces it with dirty ingredients so it will go farther, and people get abscesses from the stuff. I don't have much use for Charlie. So if I can cut in on his trade, to me it's an honor. I'm doing his customers a favor. That's why I'm here."

That settled it. This guy had to be a drug dealer. No way could he possibly be a cop.

"Now I tell you what I'm going to do," he went on. "I don't blame you for being suspicious. But I like you, and I really want to help you. So just so you can be sure I'm not a cop, I'm going to lay this bag of dope on your bench. You give me the twenty bucks, and I'll walk out that door. I know what you're worried about. You think that as soon as you have that bag of dope in your hand, I'll bust you for possession. Well, if I just lay that bag of dope down, there's no possible way I can bust you, is there?"

The guy leaned over and put his gun back in its holster. I breathed one huge sigh of relief. This guy was on the level. I couldn't wait to tell Candi. We could both get our drugs from him from now on—no more having to buy them from Martha at a higher price! And we could be sure of getting good stuff—no hot shots!

The guy laid the dope on the bench, and I handed him twenty dollars. I kept looking at the bag, hoping it really was good stuff. After all, I'd just met him. Would he rip me off? I'd have to take that chance.

As he walked out, he said, "Maybe I'll see you tomorrow. It all depends on my schedule. I really like the way you give massages. Will your two-for-one special still be on tomorrow?" He grinned.

He left, and I stood there transfixed, staring at the bag of dope and eagerly anticipating getting off. But I couldn't move too fast. What if he was just outside in the hallway, waiting for me to pick it up so he could bust me?

I left the dope sitting there, opened my door, and peered down the hall. Nobody in sight.

I threw a towel over the dope and then walked down to the reception area where Candi was sitting. "Did that little guy go out the door?" I asked her.

"Yeah," she replied, "and with a big smile on his face. What did you do to him?"

"I told you he's my cousin," I said. "I really gave him a good back rub."

"Well, I knew you must have done something. He was certainly grinning. Did he have an iron?"

"Yeah, but he's okay," I told her. "I'm sure he's not a cop. I don't want to tell you all about it now. Come to my room tonight. I may be able to tell you something then."

I hurried back to my massage room, tucked the little white packet into my pocket, and headed back upstairs. I knew Harvey would kill me if he caught me getting off during working hours, but at the moment, I didn't care. I just couldn't wait.

While in my room, I got off. The dope was good, just as the guy said. I could hardly wait for him to come back so I could get some more.

Three days went by, and still no guy came. Fortunately I

hadn't told Martha about the guy, even though I did share the good news with Candi. Candi was skeptical. I told her she'd be convinced when he came back.

It bugged me to pay Martha twenty-five dollars for stuff that wasn't as good as what the little guy sold me for twenty dollars. But it was a lot better than nothing.

Martha and I were pretty cool to each other. Our only real talking was over drug transactions. But I knew she was still seething over what I had done to her. I had to watch her!

Things really came to a head the night Dr. Vines, a regular customer, came back. As luck would have it, Martha and I were both sitting in the reception lounge when he came in. We both stood eagerly. He looked at me, then at Martha, and then back at me. I held my breath. This would be the big test. Would he choose me?

I smiled as seductively as I knew how. And so did Martha. I'd never seen her put on the charm like that before. But when he looked at her and didn't return her smile, I knew I had him. He turned to me and said, "Valarie, my little darling, I've been dreaming and waiting for this moment again."

Dr. Vines had his arm around my waist, and I turned and hugged him tight. "And would you believe I've been dreaming about you, too?" I lied. "I dreamed you and I were marooned on an island in the South Pacific—just the two of us—and we had to spend the rest of our lives there. Oh, everything was eternal bliss!"

"Beautiful! Beautiful!" he exclaimed as we walked down the hallway together.

I glanced back, and Martha was glaring at us. I knew what she was thinking. She was thinking of a way to kill me!

Since Dr. Vines seemed so enthralled with my charms, I decided to push my luck and ask for six hundred dollars. He paid me, without blinking an eye!

That night I bought four bags from Martha after we closed. I'll admit I was a little worried after the Dr. Vines deal. It would have been just like Martha to have laced the dope with rat poison! I'd have a hot shot, and that would be the end. But I had to have my dope, and that meant I'd have to take my chances.

The following morning after I got up, I got off again. As I sat there nodding, someone knocked on my door. "Who's there?" I called.

"It's me. Martha."

Martha? What did she want?

"Can I come in, Valarie?"

"Yeah, I guess so." After all, I didn't want to alienate her completely. I still needed to buy dope from her until that little guy showed again. I was a little worried about depending on him. So far he hadn't been very dependable.

When Martha opened the door, I could see she looked terrible. Her hair was unwashed, uncombed. She hadn't done anything to her face, and she was in a ragged bathrobe.

"Valarie, I know I've been pretty rough on you," she started in. "I'm sorry. We've got to work here together, so why don't we bury the hatchet. Okay?"

I didn't respond. I wondered where she was leading.

"I'm really jammed," she told me. "I was wondering if you'd mind doing me a little favor. I mean, man, my nerves are really getting the best of me this morning. Ordinarily I just take a Valium, and that straightens me out. But I've run out, and I don't think I can make it to the drugstore, feeling the way I do."

"So?" I asked.

"Listen, I've got a special account at a drugstore up on Fifty-seventh and Eighth," she went on. "Would you mind going up there and picking up the prescription for me?"

Even if Martha was holding out an olive branch, I wasn't much in the mood to do her any favors. And there were all sorts of problems with what she was asking me to do.

"Martha, you know they won't let me go in there and pick up your prescription," I protested. "I mean, those pharmacists just won't give out Valium to anybody who comes in. You'll have to do it yourself. Take a cab up there."

"Valarie, I can't face anybody when I get like this. Besides, I already called them and made arrangements for you to pick it up for me. I know the guy there. He trusts me."

"Hey, you were pretty sure I'd go, weren't you?"

"Yeah," she answered sheepishly. "I know I have no right to expect any favors after the way I've treated you. But I thought maybe if I apologized and all. Besides, I'm doing you a favor all the time in selling you dope, you know."

"Okay, okay, so maybe I owe you a favor. But even if that guy up there trusts you, that doesn't mean he'll trust me. There's no way I can go up there and pick up Valium for somebody else. If they think something's suspicious, they'll call the cops. Then I'll be in big trouble."

"Valarie, here I'm so sick I can hardly move, and I ask you one lousy little favor. Can't you go up there and—"

"Get it yourself!" I shouted. "Now get out of here and leave me alone!"

I thought I saw a tear trickle down her cheek. And she did look sick. Had I been too hard on her?

She turned to leave, but before she did, she said, "Okay, Valarie, two can play your dirty little game. But I just want to make one thing perfectly clear. From now on, your money is no good if you want to buy dope from me. I mean, the supply just completely dried up."

"Hey, Martha, calm down," I said. "We can still do business even if—"

"No way!" she replied, waving her hand. "From now on you can go out on the street and buy your own dope. And I hope you buy it from an undercover agent and get busted. Or I hope you get something that's pure milk sugar. Or I hope you get rat poison—"

"Okay, Martha, you've made your point," I said. "Now calm down. I'll go get your Valium."

"Naw, just forget it," she replied, edging out into the hall. "You're right. I'd better go get it myself. I just hope I can make it. I'm so sick."

With that she closed the door behind her. I had blown it! I didn't want to lose her as a supplier until I could be sure that little guy would come regularly. So I grabbed my coat from the chair and started for the hallway and Martha's room. It was the same old coat I used to wear when I was hustling on Times Square—thin, threadbare, and not much to keep a person warm. It occurred to me that maybe I could look for a new one while I was out this morning. With that money from Dr. Vines last night, I could get something really nice. But then, I didn't go out all that much. Maybe I didn't need a new coat. Maybe I'd better use that money to get drugs.

When I walked into Martha's room, carrying my coat, she looked up and smiled. "You win," I told her.

She was just getting her coat out of the closet. She looked at me and said, "Valarie, honey, this is a favor I'll never forget. I really mean it. You're a lifesaver. But I couldn't feel right about it if you had to walk all that way, wearing that thin little coat of yours. Here. Take my jacket. It'll keep you toasty warm on the way up to the drugstore."

Her jacket? Why would I want to wear her jacket? And why would she want me to wear it?

I stared at the outstretched jacket. Was this another of Martha's deals? Was she setting me up again? I knew I couldn't be too careful around her now!

9

"Uh, Martha, I'll be more comfortable wearing my own coat," I said. "I appreciate it and all, but—"

"I insist!" she interrupted. "If you're going to be doing this as a favor to me, the least I can do is be sure you're nice and warm."

"My coat's warm enough," I told her, not really remembering all the nights I had shivered in it and cursed the frigid winds of Times Square.

"Valarie, this coat of mine is one hundred percent nylon on the outer shell and one hundred percent nylon on the inner shell. And the insulation is eighty percent duck down and twenty percent waterfowl feathers. I mean, it's a fantastic coat."

She sounded as though she was trying to sell the coat to me, instead of just letting me wear it. But I was beginning to see it as a very inviting offer.

Yet when she pushed it toward me, I backed up. "Martha, that's too fancy a coat for me. You know, I might get out there on the street and somebody would rip me off and take your coat. I mean, anybody can tell that's a very expensive coat."

"Nonsense, Valarie. Nobody's going to rip you off. What I'm thinking about is that you have to walk clear up to

Fifty-seventh. You know how cold it gets here in Manhattan. These sidewalks between the buildings never see the sunlight. I mean, it's bitter cold out there today."

Then it hit me. I'll bet if I wore that coat, I'd be marked for something. Had Martha paid off somebody to kill me? Was that how the hit man would know whom to kill? I shuddered.

"No, Martha," I said with finality. "I'll go get your Valium for you, but I don't want to wear your coat. I'm more comfortable in my own. In fact, maybe I'll look for a new one while I'm out. Besides, your coat looks too big for me."

"Here, try it on. I'll bet it just fits you."

Before I could back away, she had the coat and was putting it on me. Would you believe it fit perfectly? Now what excuse was I going to give her?

When I started to pull it off, Martha zipped it up and said, "There. Now you just wear it. And don't worry about getting ripped off. I won't hold you responsible."

That didn't sound like Martha! So I snapped, "Look, Martha, I said I'd go after your Valium. But I won't wear your coat!"

She backed off a little and said, "Valarie, I apologize. I guess I was a little pushy over this. But I have a reason why I need you to wear this coat."

Aha! Now it was coming!

"You see," she went on, "I don't really have a legitimate prescription for Valium. But the guy at the drugstore sells it to me anyway. I mean, I do a few favors for him, if you know what I mean."

I had a pretty good idea.

"Well, sometimes that guy isn't there. So he told me if I'd always wear this coat when I picked up my Valium, he'd tell his partner that it was okay for me to get it. His partner would recognize me from the coat. So the guy told me that whatever I do, I've got to wear this coat. So that's why you've got to wear it, Valarie; they won't give you the Valium if you don't have on this particular coat."

"Martha, are you putting me on? That doesn't make too much sense, you know. Are you setting me up for something?"

"For crying out loud, you're a suspicious little snob, aren't you? Look, I know I got pretty mad at you over that Dr. Vines deal. But I'd never set you up. I'm just not that kind of a person."

"Are you positive about that?"

"Well, I guess you don't really have much of a choice, do you? If you don't go after that Valium for me, I'm going to cut off your drug supply. And if you don't wear this coat, there's no way you can get my Valium. So why don't you cut out all this nonsense, and get on your way? I've got a splitting headache, and every nerve in my body is screaming. So let's get on with it."

Maybe I was getting paranoid, seeing a setup behind every little thing that happened. I guess taking drugs has a tendency to do that to a person. It sure did to me. But Martha had spelled out my options pretty well. If I wanted to continue to buy drugs from her, I had to get her the Valium. And to get the Valium, she said I had to be wearing this particular coat. So I was taking a chance. I'd taken chances before. I'd be careful.

Besides, this coat was becoming habit-forming. I could snuggle down inside of it and laugh at those bitter winds blowing icily through the New York City canyons.

Before long I was walking up Eighth Avenue. Martha was right. It was bitter cold, and the wind was howling. But I just snuggled down into that coat and felt toasty warm.

Maybe I ought to get a coat like it. It sure beat that old thing I had been wearing.

I thrust my hands deeper into the pockets to keep my wrists warm, too. Hey! What was this? A pocket within the pocket? Maybe I could get my hands down deeper yet!

I unzipped the zipper on the inner pocket and thrust my hand down inside. No, it didn't go down any deeper, but. . . . Then I felt something down there.

I jerked my hand out and couldn't believe it. I was holding a packet of dope!

What was Martha doing with dope in her coat pocket? That didn't make sense. Or was this where she stashed some of it to keep Candi and me from stealing it? I'd noticed she changed her hiding places for the dope frequently. Obviously she didn't trust us junkies—and I couldn't blame her for that. Nobody trusts a junkie.

My conscience started telling me I ought to give the dope back to Martha. It really wasn't mine. But I'd never been one to pay much attention to my conscience. I decided it was a good case of finders keepers, losers weepers. After all, I rationalized, this would be a little bonus for my generosity in doing a favor for Martha. And she'd never even miss it. She sure wouldn't have sent me off with her coat, knowing there was a bag of dope in the pocket!

I stuffed the dope and my hand back into the pocket and checked the pocket on the other side. Nothing in it. I felt a little disappointed that I'd become the possessor of only one bag of dope.

I huddled down inside the coat to ward off the cold, but I was feeling warm inside from my good fortune. I even whistled a little tune as I made my way up Eighth Avenue.

Suddenly I got an uneasy feeling. I don't know if it was a sixth sense I developed when I was on the streets, but I felt as though I was not alone.

Oh, sure, people were coming and going all around me. Cold, frigid weather and snowstorms don't keep New Yorkers off the streets. But this was a different feeling—as though I was being followed.

I cautiously glanced back. Nobody else seemed to be paying any attention to me. Wait. Half a block away a guy was looking intently in my direction.

I took a few more steps, then wheeled around. As soon as he saw me turn, he stopped walking and acted as though he was looking in a shop window. He sure acted as though he was following me. But why?

At the next corner, rather than keeping on my direct path to Fifty-seventh, I turned right, deciding to walk over to Broadway and then double back—to see if the guy really was following me.

Halfway down that block I stopped again. Sure enough, the guy had turned the corner too. Who was he? What did he want?

I quickened my pace, deciding that when I got to the pharmacy, I'd call Martha and have her meet me there. Something was wrong with that guy, but I didn't think he'd bother me inside the drugstore.

When I headed up Broadway, the guy was still following. At Fifty-seventh I turned left. Just a block to go now.

But when I glanced ahead, I saw somebody I thought I recognized on the corner. As I got closer, I realized it was that little guy—the drug dealer—who had come in for a massage a couple of days earlier. Maybe I could make contact with him to see when he was coming in again.

He spotted me now, and he seemed to tense. What was up? What was happening?

I cut across in the middle of the block, and realized both of those dudes were tailing me now. My hand nervously squeezed the bag of dope in the pocket of Martha's coat.

The dope! That was it! That Martha had set me up! She had planted that dope in an inside pocket, figuring I'd never find it. Then she must have called the cops and told them to be on the lookout for me—that I had dope on me! What a setup!

I knew that the first thing I had to do was to get rid of that dope. Though it really pained me to get rid of a perfectly good bag of dope, it was the only way. I started running, and as I ran, I dropped the bag into a nearby trash can—without even breaking stride. I don't think the guys following me had any idea what I'd done.

When I got to the corner, I heard that little dope dealer yelling, "Halt! Halt!"

I wasn't sure what was about to happen, but I knew I couldn't get away from them. Martha's coat kept me warmer, but it was harder to run in than mine was! Maybe there were some advantages to my old, worn coat!

No sooner had I stopped than both guys grabbed me and slammed me up against the wall. The little guy said, "OK, we've got you. Now don't try anything funny."

"Hey, what in the world is going on here?" I yelled. "I was just out walking and minding my own business. I haven't done anything to you guys. Are you trying to rip off my coat?"

"Shut up! We'll do the talking!" the little guy said. "I'm Detective Canighar, and this is my partner, Detective Bristle."

In surprise I turned to face them and realized both of them were flashing badges at me. I couldn't get over it. That little drug dealer who was too small to be a cop really was a cop! Talk about dirty tricks!

The other detective started reaching into my pocket, saying, "Don't try anything funny, or you will really be in trouble!"

The way he went right for that pocket where I had found the package of dope told me instantly that that dirty Martha had set me up! She'd probably called the cops on me as soon as I walked out the door of the Blue Lagoon! Why, when I got back there, I'd kill that woman! Nobody was going to set me up like that and get by with it!

Searching all my pockets almost frantically—and unsuccessfully—the big guy spun me around and said, "Okay, girl, where's the dope?"

I stomped my foot and shouted, "All I was doing was going to the drugstore for a friend. Now if you think I've got dope on me, you go right ahead and find it!"

When they started to run their hands over my body to search me, I yelled, "You guys have no right to do that! That's against the law!"

The two guys laughed, and the little guy said, "Don't tell me you're suddenly getting squeamish about having a man touch you! That just doesn't suit your personality!"

"You know what I'm talking about!" I shot back. "That kind of a search has got to be done by a woman cop."

"Okay, okay. We got a tip that you were carrying dope in your pocket. Now what did you do with it?"

"I have no dope in my pocket," I shouted. "If you'll let me put my arms down, I'll show you."

"Okay, but do it slowly—and no tricks."

I turned every pocket inside out and finally said, "See? No dope!"

I even pulled out my blouse and said, "Take a look here if you want to."

I couldn't believe it, but the little guy looked! Oh, I was so embarrassed, especially because a small crowd had gathered and seemed to be enjoying what was going on.

Finally the little guy said, "You can go. We can't hold you. But you'd better make sure you stay clean, kid. We're on to you, and we'll get you one of these days!"

Oh, how I wanted to spit in his face. But I knew I'd better leave well enough alone.

The little guy turned to his partner and said, "It's hard to believe that some junkie like that can really give a good massage."

"You step one foot inside the Blue Lagoon," I sputtered, "and I'm going to put my hands around your throat and choke you to death!"

"Promises, promises," the little guy said, laughing, and turned to walk away.

I pushed my way through the crowd, furious for what I had been put through. I wasn't heading for any drugstore now. I was going right back to the Blue Lagoon. And when I got there, I was going to be sure that Harvey ended up with one less girl to do massages. This was Martha's last day to live!

Believe me, I made the return trip in record time. When I stomped through the front door, Martha was sitting in the reception lounge. I could tell she really was surprised to see me, and immediately she jumped up and started backing away from me.

"Martha, I'm going to kill you!" I screamed. "So help me, if it's the last thing I do, I'm going to kill you!"

I ripped her coat off me and threw it on the floor.

"Valarie! Valarie! What's gotten into you?" she asked, trying to sound innocent.

"Martha, you know exactly what happened. You set me up. The minute I left here, you called the detectives to bust me!"

"What are you talking about?"

"Don't act so innocent, Martha. You put that bag of dope in your coat pocket. That's why you wanted to be sure I wore your coat. It had nothing to do with getting that Valium!"

"Valarie, you're talking like a crazy woman!"

I brushed past her and headed for my room. I'd get my knife and stab her right through the heart. No way was anybody going to set me up and get by with it! If I had been caught with that bag of dope, I'd have been sent away for years.

I grabbed my switchblade from its hiding place under my mattress and tucked it inside my bra. Then I headed back to the reception lounge. Martha was sitting there, reading a magazine. I flicked out my switchblade and screamed, "Say your prayers, Martha! This is the day you die!"

She jumped up and pulled out her own switchblade, yelling, "You think you can do it, kid? Well, I'll even give you first chance. But if you miss, I'm going to slash your throat from ear to ear!"

I didn't respond. I just positioned my feet apart and extended my arms, waiting for an unguarded moment.

"Valarie, before you get killed," Martha yelled, "let me tell you what really happened. I didn't plant any dope in that coat. I don't know where the dope came from."

"Aw, come off it, Martha. It was in an inside pocket. You put it there. That's why you insisted I wear your coat."

"That is not!" she shot back. "If there was a bag of dope in the pocket of that coat, I had nothing to do with it. You think I'm stupid enough to send a junkie off with dope? But I think I know what happened. There was a tall detective in here, and he must have planted it."

"Quit lying, Martha!" I shot back. "You're not going to get out of this one! You've had it!"

"Valarie, please put down that knife. Let me tell you something about that coat."

"You still think I'm stupid, don't you, Martha? As soon as I put my knife away, you're going to try to slash me. I'm on to your tricks!"

"Valarie, I won't do that. Let's talk this out. Let me tell you about that coat."

"No way, Martha! You'd better say your prayers!" I brandished the knife threateningly. "I'm going to get you, and get you good!"

When she started backing away, I knew she was afraid.

"Okay, okay, just stay there, and I'll tell you anyway," she said, trying to be sure she was outside of striking range.

"I'm listening!" I snarled.

"Three days ago this big guy came in here and wanted a massage. He wanted everything, and I gave him the works. We had agreed on the price of fifty dollars. Well, he told me he was a coat salesman, and he had this coat that was worth one hundred and fifty dollars. He gave me the coat, and we called it even. I got a good deal. But now I realize something else. That guy was a detective, I bet. He planted the dope in that coat, and then staked out this place. You were the first person to walk outside wearing that coat; that's why the cops went after you. And that's the truth."

Could I believe her? Martha was full of lies. She was a quick thinker and could make her lies sound very believable. But I wasn't going to be taken in by her this time.

"You're lying! You're lying!" I screamed and made a slapping motion in her direction. She jumped back, then started circling around, her knife ready to slash.

"Put those knives down this instant!" a gruff voice ordered.

I didn't dare take my eyes off of Martha, so I yelled over my shoulder, "Harvey, Martha planted a bag of dope on me and called the cops to bust me! I'm going to kill her for that!"

"I don't care who did what!" Harvey bellowed. "Valarie, put that knife down! You, too, Martha!"

I heard a click and turned enough to see that Harvey was standing there with his gun aimed right at me!

"I said drop those knives, and I mean now!" Harvey yelled. "I've got six bullets in this magazine, and I don't mind using them on the likes of you!"

Martha's knife clattered to the floor. For a moment I considered following up my advantage, but I knew Harvey wouldn't hesitate to shoot me. And I wasn't ready to die yet!

"Valarie, drop it!" Harvey ordered, taking careful aim at me.

I slowly opened my hand, and the knife dropped. What choice did I have?

As Harvey picked up both knives, he said, "Now what on earth is going on here?"

"Martha asked me to pick up some Valium for her on Fifty-seventh Street," I said. "She insisted I wear her coat. On the way I discovered the zipper of an inner pocket and found a bag of dope down in it. About halfway there, I realized I was being tailed. Then when I got there, two cops jumped me. Only I saw what was happening and dropped the dope in a trash basket. The first thing those cops did when they grabbed me was to look in that inner pocket. And were they ever mad when they couldn't find any dope on me. Now, Harvey, you've been around a long time. You know exactly what happened on that deal. That stinking Martha set me up and called the cops to bust me. She's mad again because Dr. Vines chose me last night!"

"Lies! Lies! Lies!" Martha yelled. "I got that coat three days ago when I worked a deal with a guy. I know you don't like deals, but I got a hundred-and-fifty-dollar coat for fifty dollars. I gave you your share. Now I realize that the guy must have been a cop and planted the dope in the coat. Valarie just happened to be the first one to wear the coat outside. They must have had the place staked out, watching for that coat, don't you think?"

"She's the liar, Harvey! She's the liar!" I screamed. "She set me up, and she knows she did it. You should have seen how surprised she looked when I came back this morning! She wasn't expecting to see me again!"

"Harvey, you can't believe her," Martha argued. "She's a filthy junkie, and you know you can't trust a junkie. She stole Dr. Vines from me. And she's been ripping you off, Harvey. I've been keeping records of how many customers she's had, and I know she's holding back money that belongs to you, Harvey. You ought to take her right back to where you got her. There's been nothing but trouble here ever since she came!"

"Valarie, are you holding out on me?" Harvey asked.

"Harvey, you know I wouldn't do that to you after all you've done for me," I purred. "Think about it. Who turned over the most money to you last night?"

I knew I was safe on that one. After all, I'd got six hundred dollars from Dr. Vines. Harvey got three hundred of that!

"I'd be careful of somebody like Martha who makes that kind of accusation," I said, sidling up to Harvey. "She's probably the one who's ripping you off. I mean, she just admitted she made a deal on that coat. Did she pay you half of what it was worth? No way!"

By that point Martha was livid with rage. She stepped toward me, fists clenched. But I was ready. If she tried anything, I was going to start by scratching her eyes out!

Harvey planted himself between us and shouted, "Now both of you back up!" He pointed his gun first at Martha, then at me. "If there is any more of this nonsense, I'm going to shoot you both and throw your bodies into the river!"

I wasn't about to back up; neither was Martha. But with his gun aimed at Martha, Harvey grabbed my arm and jerked me to his office.

Still fuming I snapped, "You've got the wrong girl, Harvey. That Martha set me up!"

"Straighten her out, Harvey!" Martha called sarcastically after us. "She needs a good beating!"

It was a good thing Harvey had a firm hold on my arm and had the gun besides. I almost broke loose and headed back to get that Martha!

Harvey jerked me into his office, pushed me toward a chair and yelled, "Sit!"

I plopped into the chair, and he went around behind his desk and sat, the gun still in his hand.

"Come on, Valarie, you don't really think Martha set you up, do you?" Harvey asked, fondling the gun and not even looking at me.

"Harvey, I know you think I'm stupid about a lot of things. And maybe I am pretty naive at times. But I know Martha must have planted that dope in that coat. She even threatened me if I didn't wear it, and I tried all sorts of excuses not to wear it."

"But why would Martha set you up?"

"You know Martha, Harvey. You've been around her longer than I have. The thing that ticked her off most was that I took Dr. Vines from her. She can't admit someone can do something better than she can. She just wants me out of here so she can have him all to herself again."

"What makes you so sure?"

"Harvey, you can't trust her."

"How do you know that?"

What a perfect opening! Now I was really going to let that dirty Martha have it.

"Harvey, what would you say if I told you that one of your girls was selling drugs to the other girls and to the customers?"

He jumped up and shouted, "I'd fire her on the spot! One thing I can't afford here is somebody dealing dope. That attracts cops like you wouldn't believe. And protection here is already costing me a fortune!"

"Well, Harvey, you asked me how I know you can't trust Martha. You know you can't trust a drug dealer, and, Harvey, you've got a drug dealer right here in the Blue Lagoon."

He leaned over the desk toward me and asked, "Martha?"

I nodded.

"How do you know?"

"Harvey, don't be naive. You know I'm on the needle. You gave me a bag the first day I came in here. You know I must still be on it. Right? Where do you think I've been getting the stuff? Well, I haven't had to go out on the streets for it. From the first night I was here I've been getting my dope from Martha. And I'm not her only customer."

Harvey pounded the desk with his fists and shouted, "That weasel! I suspected what was going on, but I didn't have any proof. And she's got a lot of customers that keep coming back to see her. Are you telling me the truth?"

"Harvey, would I lie to you after all you've done for me?"

"Look, I can't trust any of you girls," he responded. "I know you're a junkie, and I can't trust a junkie anymore than I can trust a dealer. All you girls lie when you get in a corner. It's a way of life with you."

"That may be true, Harvey, but I'm not lying now."

"It's your word against hers, Valarie."

Suddenly an idea hit me—a plan I figured Harvey would go for.

"Harvey, I know it's my word against hers. But if I set something up so you can catch her red-handed, selling me dope, then you'll have to believe me. Now here's my plan. I'll get her to sell me some dope in my massage room. You have the videotape rolling, and you'll get all the evidence you need."

Harvey plopped back down into his chair. His eyes lighted up at the prospect of my suggestion, and he said, "Valarie, that's a great idea! But you'd better be sure you know what you're doing. If you blow this one, Martha may suspect you are setting her up and kill you!"

"I can take care of myself, Harvey. Don't worry."

"Well, if that Martha is selling dope in my place, I'm throwing her out on the street. Man, I can't have something like that going on in here. The cops will close me down!"

"Okay, Harvey, I'm going to go back to the lounge and apologize to Martha. Then when I get her in my room, you have that tape rolling. You're going to see a real show, Harvey. You might even be able to sell this one to the cops!"

"Hey, let's leave the cops out of this!" Harvey said nervously.

I walked straight to the reception lounge. When Martha saw me, she jumped up and started backing away.

I waved my hand toward her and said, "Cool it, Martha. I'm calmed down. I'm not going to hurt you. Harvey and I just had a long talk, and I realize what a mistake I made in accusing you of setting me up. I can see now that the stupid detective who gave you that coat was the real culprit. I'm really sorry I got so upset with you. But I guess you can see how it looked to me, with your insisting that I wear that coat and all. But I know now I jumped to the wrong conclusion. Harvey said he knew that guy was a detective. He also said that since I had caused the ruckus, I was the one who had to apologize first and make everything right between you and me. So please forgive me for all the things I said and did. I'm sorry. Okay?"

Martha blinked and gulped in surprise. "You're asking me to forgive you?"

I nodded contritely. "I made a big mistake, Martha. Come on now. Be big enough to forgive me. Please?"

"Well, I guess so."

I patted her arm and said, "Thanks, Martha." Then I whispered, "You know, what I think is really the matter with me—why I'm so edgy, so suspicious, is that I need to get off again. I got so eager when I found that bag of dope in your coat pocket. All I could think about was getting off. You can't imagine how it pained me to toss that packet into the trash on the street when the cops were after me! I mean, it was like throwing away solid gold!"

I couldn't quite tell how she was reacting. I still believed she had set that whole deal up.

"Would you let me buy a bag from you?" I asked.

"Valarie, you already got off this morning," she said. "Why do you want another bag of dope now?"

I had to think of something quick! I sure couldn't afford to blow this transaction!

10

Martha was standing there, her hands on her hips, waiting for my answer.

"Hey, I usually use two bags in the morning," I said. "You know that. I only had one. I need another."

That seemed to satisfy her.

Now I had to get the transaction in my massage room instead of upstairs.

"You know, Martha," I whispered, "I get the distinct feeling that Harvey has my room bugged upstairs. I don't think he really trusts me yet. He said something once about trust being something you earn. Do you know if he has any rooms bugged?"

"Harvey bug those rooms? Are you kidding?"

"Well, it seems to me he's very suspicious of us girls," I said. "And I know he's paranoid about drugs around here."

"Well, you're right about that," Martha answered. "But I think it's best to do our drug transactions upstairs. I get leery of doing business down here."

"Hey, just this once couldn't we do it back in my room down here?" I asked. "Harvey's likely to get suspicious if we're both upstairs since Candi and Cindy aren't here. We need to be here—at least one of us. You could go up and get the stuff, and then we could make the deal back in my room. That way Harvey won't suspect a thing. Okay?"

Martha hesitated a moment, as if weighing the consequences. Then she nodded and said, "I'll be right back."

I waited a few moments and then walked back to my room. I couldn't believe how readily I had talked her into it. I thought she was smarter than that!

When she sneaked into my room a few minutes later, I looked at her hand. There was the packet of dope, partially hidden.

I pulled out a twenty and a five and pushed them in her direction. But instead of taking the money, she backed toward the wall—the wall where all those blacks dots were. Oh, no! She knew what she was doing! She stood right against the wall with her back covering the camera lens! This gal knew exactly what she was doing. And there was no way I could get the proof I so desperately needed.

Wordlessly she motioned me over to where she stood.

"What in the world are you doing?" I asked.

She kept motioning me closer, still not talking. Instead she pointed over her shoulder at the lens and motioned as though she were locking her lips.

This just wasn't working as I had planned.

I didn't dare make an issue. She knew that Harvey could tape anything in these rooms, and she wasn't taking any chances.

When I walked up to her, she said, "Now, Valarie, when you give a massage, be sure to concentrate on the muscles on the side."

Smart! She was covering herself. She knew the sound was picked up in this room, too!

With her back still against the wall, covering the camera lens, she held out the dope. I gave her the money and stuffed the bag into my jeans.

As she started for the door, she said, "Valarie, if you'll

remember those instructions, you'll do a good job, and you'll have a lot of repeat customers. That's where you'll really make the dough—from the repeaters."

Then she disappeared out the door and back down the hall.

I had blown it. There was no way Harvey could get that deal on tape.

Disappointed and discouraged, I headed for Harvey's office. He was waiting for me.

I showed him the bag of dope and said, "I know this really doesn't prove anything. That Martha was a lot smarter than I gave her credit for being. She backed up against the wall and covered the camera lens. So it's still my word against hers."

"No it isn't!" Harvey exploded. "I ought to kill that Martha! I mean, I ought to kill her! I didn't think she'd ever do anything like this to me! I bailed that girl out of jail and fixed it so she didn't have to appear in court. I gave her a good job and a place to stay. And then she turns on me and is selling dope. I mean, I ought to kill her."

"Well, that's what I was trying to do for you, Harvey," I reminded him. "If you hadn't interfered, she'd be dead by now. But what made you decide to believe me?"

Harvey took his keys and unlocked a drawer. I peered over the desk and saw a bunch of dials.

"I'm going to tell you something, Valarie," he said, "something I haven't told any of the other girls. But I guess I can trust you. You were right about this deal. See all these knobs here? I have hidden microphones in every room in this place. I mean, every room."

This Harvey was really into electronic gadgetry.

"I've got two reasons for this," Harvey went on. "First, I want to know every customer who comes in here. If one of you girls gets into trouble in your room and can't even call for Angelo, I can monitor and know what's going on. That way I can bust in with my gun if there's trouble.

"My second reason ought to be quite obvious. I've told you I can't trust you girls. Well, I'm not about to let you rip me off. Since we don't have set fees, I have to know what kind of deals the girls are making, so I know how much of a cut I'm supposed to get from them each night. I keep my records. And I've noticed that not once have you tried to rip me off."

I made a mental note never to try it either. This Harvey was too smart.

"When you left here a few minutes ago," he went on, "I flipped on the mike out in the reception lounge. I heard all the conversation there. I know Martha went up to her room. I heard her muttering to herself there. I know she covered the TV lens in your massage room. But why would she have come to your room after that if it wasn't to sell you the dope? And you did end up in here with that bag."

Harvey ran his fingers through his greasy hair and looked blankly at me, as if pondering his next move. Then he pulled out my switchblade and handed it across the desk. "I think she set you up this morning," he said. "I don't know why, but I think she did. If I were you, I'd kill her!"

I grabbed the switchblade and asked, "You really want me to do her in?"

"Somebody's got to," Harvey replied. "And I think you'd better do it before she does you in. I'm going to tell you something, Valarie. This whole thing has hurt me deeply. But any girl who would come in here and start selling dope after all I've done for her is capable of anything. I know she planted that dope and called the cops. In fact, while you were out this morning, she made a statement that didn't make sense then. But it does now. She said something about how you had gone out and you looked as though you didn't plan to come back!"

That did it! I was convinced too that she had set me up. I was going to get that Martha, and get her good!

"She's pretty good with a knife," I said. "You think I can get her first?"

"Yeah, she's not as good as she claims to be," Harvey responded. "But you've got to be careful when someone else has a knife."

"Well, you've got her knife," I said. "But I think she keeps a spare in her massage room. We can be pretty sure she's gone after it by now."

Harvey nodded. He didn't know what I was thinking about doing to him.

"Harvey, you've got to trust me about something," I said.

"Valarie, I told you I never trust my girls."

"Harvey, if we're going to be sure we get Martha out of the way, I'm going to need your gun."

Without a moment's hesitation he pulled out his gun and handed it to me. Now I knew he really wanted Martha out of the way!

My hand trembled a little as I took the gun from his grasp. I'd never killed anyone before. Would I have the nerve to do it?

I started thinking about what Martha had done to me—and how I'd be doing years and years if I hadn't found that dope before the cops did. Fuming inside, I headed for the reception lounge, gun in one hand, switchblade in the other. I'd teach that Martha to tangle with me!

When I got out there, only Candi was sitting there. She took one look at the knife and gun and jumped backward. "Valarie, are you okay?" she asked cautiously.

"Yeah, I'm fine. Where's Martha?"

"Funny you should ask. A couple of minutes ago she headed out the door wearing that new coat of hers. All she said to me was, 'It's been nice knowing you.' I didn't pay any attention to that."

"Did she say when she'd be back?"

"No. When she waved good-bye, I thought she was acting strangely. I went to the door to call something after her, and she was running down the street."

Candi didn't have to tell me anything else. Martha had suspected what was happening and took off.

I ran outside and looked up one way and down the other. No Martha anywhere! That dirty, stinking creep! She was gone. That was lucky for her, because I was mad enough to kill her!

Harvey had followed me and saw me standing on the sidewalk with the gun and the knife. He grabbed me and pulled me back inside. "Hey, don't be stupid with those things!" he said. "You want to frighten away customers and get all the cops in the neighborhood aroused?"

He took the gun from me and slipped it under his belt. "Keep the blade," he said. "You may need it sometime."

Then he went back outside to see if he could spot where Martha had gone. Moments later he came back in and told me to sit on the sofa in the lounge. "Listen, there's a big customer coming," he said. "You give him your best smile when he comes in. I called him and told him I had a special deal for him. We'll worry about Martha later. I can put out a contract on her."

I shuddered a little as I thought about Harvey's power over us girls. When he got through with us, it apparently meant nothing to him to have us killed! What a mess I'd gotten into.

When the fat guy came in moments later, I gave him my most beguiling smile.

"Hey, Harvey called me about a special deal," he said. "You know anything about it?"

A big diamond sparkled in his ring as he gestured. This guy obviously had money!

"Mister, every day at the Blue Lagoon is a special day," I cooed. "I mean, real special! Want the works?"

He grinned and said, "I'll take everything you've got, kid!"

As I led him to my room, I was wondering what special Harvey had in mind. Before I tried anything, I'd better check. So I pointed the guy to my table and said, "Why don't you go in and get yourself comfortable? I'll go get what Harvey called you about."

I hurried to Harvey's office and stuck my head in the door. "Hey, I got this rich one who said you called him. What's up?"

Harvey pushed a tin can toward me.

"What's that?"

Harvey laughed. "You'll never believe the name."

I took the can and opened it. "It looks like car grease," I said. "What is it?"

"It's called Tingling Tahiti."

"Tingling Tahiti? What in the world is that?"

"Just put a little on your arm and rub. You'll see."

As I rubbed the stuff into my arm, it felt warm. Then it began to tingle. Harvey rubbed some on his arm. "Isn't that fantastic?" he asked. "That's a real zinger!"

"Where'd it come from?" I asked.

"I got it down on Forty-second Street—saw it in the window of a shop. I really don't believe in things like that, but the guy told me to try it. When he put some of it on my arm, I got this wild idea that the stuff would go great in my massage parlor. I picked you, Valarie, to be the first one to use it. I called Harold Zolet, one of my old customers. He's kooky and likes different things. So, baby, he's yours."

I took the little can and headed back to my room. This was going to be interesting!

When I opened the door, Harold stood there in his shorts. "Tell me what the big deal is," he said. "Harvey sounded as though it was the biggest thrill a person could have."

I pointed to the can and said, "In this little can, Mr. Zolet, is an experience you will never forget. Harvey calls it Tingling Tahiti."

"Tingling Tahiti?"

"Yeah," I replied. "I really can't explain it. It's something you're going to have to experience. I mean, you're going to go into orbit over this. You're going to tingle all over as though you were in Tahiti—Tahiti in the summer instead of New York City in the winter!"

"Well, I'm ready for something new," he said. "And if it'll help me forget the winter outside, so much the better. Harvey's never disappointed me yet, so let's go at it, kid."

As he eased onto the massage bench, I noticed his watch—absolutely exquisite, with diamonds encircling the face and studded down the band. Wouldn't I like to get hold of that!

I rubbed some of the stuff into his back and then started down his arms.

"Wow! This is great!" Harold said. "That really is invigorating."

"Here, let me rub it all over your arms," I said. "Maybe we ought to take off your watch. I'll put it here on my stand."

Without any hesitation he slipped the watch off. Momentarily I held it, admiring those big diamonds. If I could just figure out a way to steal it—but it would sure be obvious who took it!

As I rubbed both his arms, Harold began to squirm even more. "Hey, this is heavenly!" he exclaimed. "Has Harvey had this all the time?"

I sure didn't want to tell him that Harvey got it on Forty-second Street. There were some real wackos there selling nothing but junk.

When I put some more on his back, he started letting out little squeaks. He was totally enjoying this.

Then the door of my room opened, and there stood Harvey. Shutting the door behind him, he walked over and said, "What do you think, Harold?"

"Harvey, you should have told me about this before! I mean, man, I'd pay a bundle for this. I'm going to give this girl a hundred bucks for this rub. This Tingling Tahiti is really it!"

As I kept rubbing, Harvey glanced around the room. Then he said, "Harold, close your eyes. Visualize yourself in Tahiti. See the palm trees swaying in the summer breeze. You're lying there on the beautiful, warm sand, and the waves are lapping at the shore. Five beautiful native girls are caressing and rubbing you."

Harold closed his eyes and smiled dreamily.

"I'm going to turn out the light," Harvey went on, "to shut out this room completely and help you fantasize. I mean, it will send you into orbit!"

When Harvey clicked off the light, I kept rubbing gently. Harold kept squirming. Then I noticed Harvey leave.

A little while later I finished with the massage and went over and turned on the lights. Harold sat up on the bench, yawned, and then reached for his watch. That's when I heard him bellow, "Where's my watch?"

It was gone! I sure didn't have it. That must be why Harvey turned out the lights. But Harold wouldn't think that his old buddy Harvey had taken it. That left me as the prime suspect.

"Come on, girl; give me back my watch!" Harold yelled. "That's a pretty good scheme, turning out the lights so you could rip off my watch. Now give it back to me before I choke it out of you!"

"Hey, calm down, will you?" I yelled back. "I didn't steal your watch. I have no idea where it is."

Harold jumped off the bench and grabbed my blouse. Drawing me up close, he threatened, "Listen, girl, that watch is worth twenty-five hundred dollars! And I'm sure not letting any little massager rip it off. Now give it back!"

"Hey, Mr. Zolet, you've got no problem with me," I responded. "I didn't steal your watch."

Before I could pull away he had his hand inside my blouse, digging and searching. "Not there. Where have you hidden it?"

"Listen, Mr. Zolet, I don't have your watch. The last time I saw it was when you handed it to me, and I put it on that little stand. When I turned on the light, I was as surprised as you to discover it was gone."

"You're a lying witch!" he yelled. "And I'm going to kill you for this!" He kept screaming, "Where is my watch? Where is my watch?"

"I don't have your watch!" I shouted. "You know I was standing right there, rubbing you the whole time the lights were out."

He grabbed his undershirt, pulled it over his head, and shouted, "Okay, girl. I don't know if you took it or if Harvey took it. But I'm going to leave now. And I'm going to be back here within an hour. If I don't get my watch back, there's going to be a dead body in here—yours!"

He sounded so sinister that my heart started beating wildly.

"Mister, please," I begged. "Don't make threats like that. I didn't take your watch."

"So maybe you didn't rip me off," he admitted. "I don't know for sure. But there is one thing I am sure of, girl. That watch was here in your room on your stand. Now it's gone. And since this is your room, that makes you responsible for my watch. So if you've got to sell your body, or soul, or whatever, you'd better get that watch back and have it waiting for me when I come back here in an hour. You understand?"

All this time he was jabbing his finger right into my face. There was no question in my mind that he meant business.

After he headed out the front door, I stomped down to Harvey's office. I didn't even bother to knock. I just shoved the door open and demanded, "Okay, Harvey, where is it?"

"Where is what?"

"Where is Harold's watch?"

"Come on, Valarie, you're not going to try to pull that one on me, are you?" he said disgustedly. "That's one of the oldest ones in the book. You rip off Harold's watch and then accuse me of doing it. Now when I left your room, I saw his watch still on your stand. In fact, when I went out into the hall from the darkened room, I looked back and noticed the diamonds sparkling from the hall light."

I didn't know if he could or not, but I really wasn't in a position to argue.

"There's no way I'd do something like that, Valarie, not to Harold or any of my customers. I run an honest business. I expect to see these guys coming back again. Do you think they'd keep coming back if I ripped them off? Of course not. Use your head. I don't want someone calling the cops and creating a big scene and all."

"I didn't say you took it," I said quietly. "All I know is that Mr. Zolet says he doesn't have his watch. He's coming back here in an hour, and he wants it back then."

Slamming his fist on his desk, Harvey roared, "Are you accusing me of stealing?"

"Look, Harvey, I'm not accusing you of anything. I just know Mr. Zolet made some terrible threats about killing me if I don't have his watch back to him in an hour."

"You'd better believe Harold will make some threats. And he's likely to make good on them. You know who he is?"

"Of course not. I've never seen him before," I replied.

"Harold owns six porno shops down in the Times Square area and is reputed to be a member of the mob. He could easily put out a contract on your life if you don't return his watch. That watch cost him more than a contract on your life would cost!"

"Harvey, I don't have that watch!" I screamed, as the horror of the situation began to sink in.

"You're in deep trouble," Harvey said, confirming my fears. "In an hour Mr. Zolet will come back, just as he said. But he won't be alone. He'll have a couple of his goons. They'll probably rip your arms off. They may even slam a couple of bullets into your brain. I mean, Valarie, you had better get that watch back to him pronto. You picked the wrong guy to pull this on."

"Harvey, how many times do I have to tell you that I don't have that watch? You're the only other person who was in there. Now what did you do with it?"

Harvey jerked open the desk drawer, and once again I was staring at the business end of his pistol. "Valarie, don't you even think about accusing me of taking that watch. You didn't tell Mr. Zolet that I took it, did you?"

"Of course not. I've got my ethics."

"Mr. Zolet is a smart man," Harvey told me. "Maybe he's setting you up for something. Did you watch to be sure he didn't take the watch and stick it in his own pocket—and then accuse you of stealing it? That's been tried before too."

"Harvey, I don't think the man is that good an actor," I said. "He seemed genuinely surprised and upset when his watch was gone."

I really hadn't thought of the possibility of Mr. Zolet's stealing his own watch. But I didn't think that was what had happened. What I suspected was that Harvey saw it as a good chance to get an expensive watch—and finger me. And who was going to take the word of a massager-junkie that she didn't steal a watch like that!

"I'm going to go back to my room and search it thoroughly," I announced. "It might have fallen onto the floor or something. But I'm telling you something, Harvey. If he comes back here with a couple of goons, they're going to start tearing this place to pieces. And after they get me, they're going to come after you!"

"Now look who's threatening who!" Harvey said sarcastically. "You don't scare me. I know Mr. Zolet. He knows me and trusts me. And he also knows that all you girls are a bunch of dirty, filthy liars. And you junkies are the worst of the lot. Nobody's going to believe the word of a junkie!"

Trembling all over I returned to my room. In less than an hour I was going to confront the mob. I had heard that those guys had no mercy.

I looked under the massage bench, the top of the table, a little drawer in it. It wasn't anywhere in my room. It had to be that Harvey had ripped it off and had decided to let me take the heat for it.

I glanced at my own watch nervously—less than thirty minutes before he came back.

I headed back to the reception lounge at front, hoping some customers would stop by. Nobody came in, though, and I was alone with my thoughts.

It was only ten more minutes now. I had to do something quickly. But what?

Suddenly the front door burst open, and there stood two giants who reminded me a lot of Angelo. They both stared at me menacingly. This was going to be the end!

11

Why had I waited around? I should have gotten out while there was time. Now there was no way I could get out that door. And those two gangster-type goons blocking my way were killers. I had no doubt of that!

Maybe I could bluff. After all, how would they know which girl Mr. Zolet thought took his watch? I wasn't the only girl working at the Blue Lagoon.

With a great deal more boldness than I felt I started toward the front door. "I thought I'd take a look to see if one of my customers was coming," I said. "He called a little while ago, and I'm surprised he isn't here yet. Mind if I take a look?"

One guy held out his arm to block my way, and he shook his head that I wasn't to go outside. Well, I sure wasn't going to argue with him. Both these characters looked like Angelo.

Angelo? Hey, that was it! Angelo was here to protect me. If I ever needed protection, it was now!

I yelled his name as loud as I could, startling the two guys. In a moment I heard the heavy stomp of Angelo's feet running toward me. When he came into sight, I just pointed toward the two goons.

Angelo stopped short, looked, and growled like an animal. This was going to be a real fight!

One of the goons yelled, "Hey, don't try anything funny, or it'll be the last thing you try!"

That was like saying "sic 'em" to a dog. Angelo growled and grimaced and stepped toward the two. I edged closer to the door. This might be an interesting fight, but I had no intention of standing around and watching it. As soon as they tangled, I was heading out that door! So it was cold, and I didn't have a coat. I'd worry about that later!

"Listen, you dumb gorilla," one of the goons said. "I'd really hate to splatter you all over this room. It ain't going to look nice when I'm through with you."

Angelo snarled and growled and moved another step closer. I just knew that in another moment I'd be out that door. These people were not going to pin the rap on me for stealing some watch. That was Harvey's problem.

"You think I'm kidding, gorilla?"

With that he reached inside his coat and pulled out a pistol that he aimed right at Angelo's heart! "This will blast a hole in you big enough to drive a car through!" he snarled. "Now I'd suggest that you go quietly back to your cage."

This had ceased to be a fair fight! I knew the guy wouldn't think twice about blasting Angelo. And I didn't think that Harvey would trust Angelo with a gun.

Angelo, however, wasn't about to give up. He had his job to do, and he was willing to do it. He growled again and yelled, "Mister, you put one hand on Valarie, and that will be last girl you touch!"

That gun had changed my plans to try to get out the door. Even if I did succeed—which was doubtful—the guy would put a bullet in my back.

Angelo looked at me for his orders. I knew that if the poor guy tackled those two goons, they would make mince-meat out of him. He was no match for their weapons. But if

I told him to fight, he'd do it and probably get killed. Much as I disliked all Angelo stood for, I felt kind of motherly toward him. And in that moment, I knew I couldn't let him get hurt on my account.

"Everything's okay now, Angelo," I told him softly. "You can go back to your room. If I need you again, I'll yell."

"I take them if you want me to, Valarie," he said. "Angelo not scared."

"Nobody said you were scared, Angelo."

"Did they hurt you?" he asked.

"No, nobody hurt me," I replied.

"Naw, I didn't hurt this little girl," the big guy said, smiling. "But I'd sure like to get a back rub from her."

Maybe that was my answer! "Mister," I said, "you look like you could use a back rub. I mean, I'll give you one you'll never forget. How about it?"

He giggled and said, "How about a rain check? The boss told me I was to stand by this door and make sure nobody left. But the next time I come here, I'll pick you out, little girl. You look like you're a great massager!"

Well, the back rub wasn't going to work either. I'd have to think of something else. But I figured I'd better start by getting rid of Angelo. His presence could explode this situation.

"Angelo, Valarie wants you to go back to your room now," I said. "I will yell if I need you. Okay?"

He turned and lumbered back down the hall, the walls shaking from his tread. I breathed a little easier—for his sake. But my heart was beating like crazy—for my sake. It was evident that these goons weren't going to hurt me immediately. They were just here to make sure I didn't go anywhere.

One of them stayed and guarded the door while the other

one headed for Harvey's office. I didn't see any point in sitting there staring at the big character, so I headed for my
room. In the hallway Candi motioned me into her room.

"Valarie, something strange is going on in this place!"
she whispered.

I raised my eyebrows.

"You won't believe this, Valarie. I just had this rich guy
in my room—somebody Harvey called about a special he
had. Harvey gave me a can of stuff called Tingling Tahiti to
put on him. The guy was wearing an expensive watch, so I
put it on the stand over there." She pointed. "While I was
giving the guy the massage, Harvey comes in to ask him
how he likes it. Then Harvey tells him to imagine he's in
Tahiti and turns out the light and goes out. Well, when I
get through and turn the light back on, the guy's watch is
gone. I mean, it was an extremely expensive watch—diamonds and everything. Would you believe that dumb Harvey tried to pin the rap on me?"

"What?" I yelled. "Did Harvey pull that on you, too? He
did the same thing to me!"

"I don't know what that dumb jerk was thinking of,"
Candi went on. "But he's not going to outsmart me. I got
out of it."

"You got out of it? How?" I asked eagerly. "I'm right in
the middle of it now."

"Well, Valarie, I talked my way out of it. I don't see why
you can't do that too."

"Listen, Candi, right now there's a mob-type goon
guarding the front door and another back in the office
talking to Harvey. The guy I had owns several porno shops
and either has mob connections or operates the same way."

"I see. You do have a problem," Candi responded. "All I
did when my guy came back, yelling and screaming, was to
say, "Listen, mister, if I were you, I'd call the cops!"

"What did he say? What did he do?"

"Do? What could he do?" Candi responded. "Oh, he laughed a little. He knew that if he came in here with the cops, all I would have to do would be to call the newspapers. Let me tell you something else about this guy. He didn't just get a back rub from me. He looked like a businessman. So he had nothing on me, and I had everything on him. You know what I mean?"

I nodded.

"Now I wish there was some way I could get a cut out of what Harvey gets for that watch," Candi said wistfully. "But I hope he doesn't pull that one again. It's a pretty stupid trick."

"You can say that again," I chimed in. "And I don't have your luck, Candi. I didn't get an ordinary businessman. And now this guy is threatening to kill me if I don't give him back his watch. Oh, Candi, what am I going to do?"

Just then we heard a blood-curdling scream come from Harvey's office. Candi and I ran in that direction, and from the inside Harvey was yelling, "I didn't take it! I didn't take it! I didn't take it!"

Just then the office door flew open, and the goon brushed past us. Harvey was holding his right hand, screaming and groaning and cursing.

The goon stomped down the hall to the front entrance, motioned to the other guy, and the two of them left. I was safe—at least for now.

"Valarie, get in here now!" Harvey screamed. "Right now!"

Candi took off. She didn't want to be a part of this massacre!

Harvey was bent over, holding his right hand in his left, screaming and cursing. He raised his head slightly and shouted at me, "Get in here right now I said! Get in here before I kill you!"

When I walked in, Harvey asked, "Do you know what that goon just did to me?"

He held out his hand. "Here. Look at this."

I noticed two of his fingers bent out of shape.

"He didn't!" I gasped.

"Oh, but he did," Harvey replied grimacing in pain. "He broke my fingers!"

I almost said, "Good for you! Maybe that'll teach you not to do something so stupid as to steal watches." But I knew Harvey had a gun and wouldn't hesitate to use it on me if it served his purposes. I'd better play it cool.

"I know what you're talking about!" I replied. "When those goons came in, I called Angelo. One of them pulled a gun and threatened to kill him, and to kill me, too. They're mean dudes. You really think your fingers are broken?" I reached out to touch them.

Harvey yanked them away and yelled, "Of course they're broken! That's why those characters came here. And he said that when he comes back, he's going to break my neck. I believe him! I believe him!"

"Why didn't you give him the watch?" I asked.

"What? You think I'm crazy? If I gave him that watch, then they really would come and shoot me. You don't mess around with the mob."

I wondered if Harvey had realized I had tricked him into admitting he had taken the watch.

"Harvey, you know what you just admitted? I know I didn't take the watch. Now you're saying you've got it. You're admitting you took it, aren't you?"

"Now just calm down, Valarie. I didn't tell those guys that I took the watch, and I didn't tell them that you took it."

"What?"

"I didn't admit anything about who took the watch," he went on. "All they said was that they were going to be back in an hour. The guy was giving me an hour to think things over. They said they were going to get that watch back one way or another."

"Harvey, you've really gotten yourself into a mess on this one," I said. "Why did you do something so stupid?"

He pulled the watch out of a drawer, handed it to me, and said, "Here, Valarie, you can have it."

I jumped back. "Wait a minute, man! You just got through telling me you didn't give them the watch because if you did, they'd kill you. No way am I going to put my hands on that watch and get myself killed!"

"Valarie, you've got to help me out of this one," Harvey pleaded. "If you don't, you're going to be in deep trouble, too. Now you take that watch and give it to them when they come back."

"You really think I'm stupid, don't you, Harvey? No way am I going to give those goons that watch. They're not going to splatter me all over this joint!"

"Valarie, you're not reading this one right," Harvey went on. "You'll probably get off. You're a girl. Besides, you can give them some free service. Give them ten free massages—the whole works. And I know you, Valarie. After the first massage and the works, they'll forget about the problem with the watch. Come on. You've got to do this for me."

Harvey was smart. But I wasn't about to fall for his ruse. It was his mess. He'd made it. Let him clean it up.

"Nice try, Harvey, but get yourself another patsy."

I wheeled around and walked out. "Halt right where you are!" Harvey ordered. But I kept on walking.

When I heard a gunshot, I hit the floor. By the time I

rolled over, there stood Harvey, his gun in his left hand, but pointed right at my head.

"Valarie, apparently you don't understand something about this operation," Harvey said. "When I make a request of my employees, it's more than a request. I'm just being polite to phrase it as a request. It's an order. Now you get up and march back into my office and get that watch off my desk. March!"

I was looking straight into the barrel of the gun. I'd say that Harvey really knew how to make a point in an argument!

"Get up!" he screamed again.

I slowly rolled over and headed back to his office. I didn't want to get my fingerprints on the watch, so I picked it up gingerly with my little finger. Harvey still had the gun aimed at me. But I thought I would test him. So I said, "Suppose I don't give them the watch. Suppose I just take off with it. Then where would that leave you?"

"Valarie, you're absolutely stupid. All I'd have to do is tell them you had it and had taken off. They'd believe me because you were gone. And they would turn heaven and earth upside down to find you and kill you. You'd never have a good night's sleep again!"

"Harvey, I just can't understand you," I said, balancing the watch on my little finger. "I mean, man, it was stupid of you to take that watch. Any little kid could have figured out who took it. You turned out the lights, you left, and the watch was missing. It doesn't take Sherlock Holmes to figure that out. There's no way you can get out of it. It was stupid, really stupid. I thought you had more brains than that!"

I could see Harvey was still in intense pain. But that didn't keep him from bellowing, "Valarie, I'm not going to stand here and take all this nonsense from you. I know what I'm doing. I take a little chance now and then. I saw that watch, and I knew it was valuable. Usually there's not much problem in ripping off people who come in here. There's nothing they can do about it. But I forgot momentarily who Harold was. So I made a little mistake. Lots of people make mistakes. But we're going to get out of this. And next time I'll be a little more careful."

I was so thoroughly disgusted I wanted to snap the gun out of Harvey's hand, turn it on him, and just take off with the watch. I didn't know how much I could get if I pawned it, but I knew it must be extremely valuable.

"Now take the watch and go to your room," Harvey said. "When they come, I'll direct them to your room. Everything will be okay. Just trust me."

No way was I going to trust Harvey! And I didn't plan to get torn up by a couple of goons.

But it wasn't settling anything to be here arguing with Harvey. Besides, he wasn't very steady using that gun with his left hand. There was no telling what might happen!

I walked to my room, shut the door behind me, went over to the bench, and sat down. I studied the beautiful watch, still dangling from my finger. Then I let it slide onto my stand—the place from which it had disappeared to cause all this trouble.

Now what was I going to do? It wouldn't be long before those goons were back. I started pacing the room. Every once in a while I'd stare at the watch. It really was stunning. Maybe if I left it there, someone else would steal it!

That gave me an idea, so I headed back to the reception lounge. Candi was sitting there and looked up when she saw me. "That bullet hit you?" she asked.

Then she started to laugh. I didn't think it was at all

funny. "Does Harvey always take shots at his girls?" I asked.

"Yeah, about once a week. But he hasn't killed any of us—at least, not yet!"

"Candi, I'm really in a jam. Will you help me out?"

"Sure. You want me to buy a watch?"

"Hey, come on. This is serious! Those goons are coming back in an hour, and somehow I've got to get out of this one."

"Why don't you do what I did—talk your way out of it."

I wanted to slap her for treating the whole thing so lightly. Did she know what it was like to face death?

"Candi, I want you to make up a story for me," I said. "I want you to take the watch. When those two guys come in, you tell them you found it underneath the table. Just hand them the watch, and that will be it."

"You think I'm stupid, Valarie? Didn't you see the size of those characters? They could kill me!"

"I don't think they'll do that, Candi. They know you weren't involved. Besides, I'll give you five hundred bucks if you do this for me!"

"Well, that isn't very much for putting my life and limbs on the line," she replied slowly. "But for seven hundred and fifty bucks—"

"Hey, Candi, don't jam me up against the wall. Five hundred is my top price, and it's going to take a little doing for me to get that much together. Come on, five hundred bucks—cash."

"Why not?" she said. "For a good friend like you, I'll do it for five hundred."

I might as well have promised her seven hundred and fifty dollars. I didn't have five hundred dollars either. But maybe Dr. Vines could let me borrow it from him. Or maybe I could pull something spectacular that he'd be willing to pay a grand for!

I went back to my room, got the watch with my little finger, and carried it back to Candi. The moment she saw it, she snatched it away, exclaiming, "Wow! This must be really expensive! Are those real diamonds?"

Candi was turning the watch over admiringly, putting her fingerprints all over it. But I really didn't care what she did with it. At least, it was out of my care—and now maybe I'd be able to live.

"I think I'll just take off with this," she said, "and. . . ."

That would never do. If she took off with it, the mob would assume that I still had it, and they'd come after me. So I grabbed her arm and warned, "Candi, don't you even think of pulling a trick like that. When the guys come in, I'll tell them you took off with it. And they'll follow you forever until they find you and kill you."

"Well, since this involves quite a risk and a lot of danger," Candi said, "I think that at least you ought to pay me the five hundred bucks in advance—right now!"

"Come on, Candi; be reasonable. You know I don't have that kind of cash right this minute. But I'll get it. I've got good customers."

"Promises, promises, promises," Candi sneered. "Any money you get, you shoot up in dope immediately."

"Look who's talking!" I snapped. When I saw her bristle, I knew I needed to back off. I had to have her help.

"You've got my word I'll pay you that money, Candi," I said, regaining control of my emotions.

I wasn't sure how I was going to do it. But the thought crossed my mind that if the goons killed me, I wouldn't have to worry about paying Candi! And five hundred bucks in exchange for my life seemed like a pretty good bargain.

"Okay, Valarie. I know you're in a jam. But so help me, if you don't give me that five hundred bucks soon, I'm going to tell those gangsters exactly what happened—about how you stole the watch. So you'd better play it right with me, or you're in big trouble!"

"Look, Candi, you've got my word."

I turned and walked back to my room. But every few steps I'd glance over my shoulder. If Candi took off with that watch, I was leaving, too.

From my room I heard the front door open. Even before I heard them speak, I knew it had to be those goons from Mr. Zolet. How would Candi handle it?

I walked over close to my door where I could hear without being seen.

"Gentlemen, it's good to see you again," I heard Candi tell them. "And I have some good news for you. While you were gone and I was sitting here, I happened to glance under that table over there and saw something sparkle. I walked over and looked closer. It was a watch—an expensive watch, with lots of diamonds. Now I understand that the man you work for lost an expensive watch. Would this happen to be it by any chance? It looks like the one you were describing."

Good old Candi!

"Hey," one of the goons said excitedly, "the boss is going to be happy! We got his watch!"

"Then this is the watch you were looking for?" Candi asked.

"Yeah, that's it."

"It looks like a very expensive watch," she went on. "I'll bet there's a big reward for the person who finds it. Right?"

That stupid Candi! Why didn't she quit while she was still ahead?

I heard a resounding smack. That confirmed my suspicions that she should have kept her mouth shut.

"Don't get smart with us!" I heard one of the goons say. "We'll be back!"

The front door slammed, and I headed down to the reception lounge. There was Candi holding her mouth. I could see the blood trickling out of the corners and over her fingers. As soon as she saw me, she yelled, "Valarie, don't you ever ask me for another favor—ever! I almost got killed!"

"You got off easy!" I responded. "Those guys are killers. They don't usually stop with slapping someone around!"

"I should have told them you took the watch, Valarie! I should have told them!"

"I didn't take that stupid watch!" I yelled back. "That jerk Harvey took it. But he was afraid that if he gave it back to them, they'd kill him. That's what that shot was about. Harvey forced me to take the watch and give it back to them."

"Yeah, but you didn't tell me they might beat up on me when I just did a simple little thing like give them their watch back."

"Listen, Candi, I heard what went on. And you did a very stupid thing in asking for a reward. Those guys were mad as hornets over this whole deal. They weren't about to give any reward when they knew somebody in this place had tried to rip off their boss. If you'd learn to keep your mouth shut and just leave well enough alone, well—"

"I don't need any lectures from you!" Candi exploded. "Now give me that five hundred dollars you agreed on."

"Candi, we've already been through that. I don't have that kind of money yet. But I'll get it. Just be patient. I'll get it."

She skulked down the hall toward her room. I could see her lip and mouth were really bleeding now. Would she have to have stitches for that injury? I figured I hadn't heard the end of this yet from her.

No sooner had she disappeared into her room than Harvey walked out to where I was. "Did the guys get their watch?" he asked.

I noticed his hand was wrapped in a bandage, but he was still rubbing it.

"Yeah, they got it. But when they left, they said they were coming back. What do you think that means?"

"Valarie, you're stupid. They're taking the watch back to Harold. Then they're coming back after you!"

"Harvey, don't say things like that. I'm scared enough!" I looked him square in the eye and said, "Besides, you're the one who took that watch and started this mess!"

Harvey snickered. "Valarie, nobody will believe that. Why would an honest businessman like me try to rip somebody off—especially when he's a good customer, and he knows that I know he's got mob connections. Harold Zolet knows I'm not stupid enough to pull something like that. No way."

He paused. "I heard that little deal you worked out with Candi," he went on. "Pretty clever, weren't you? You thought you'd let her take the fall for you."

I nodded. "I'm paying her," I said.

"Yeah, but she doesn't have the money yet. And you're not likely to get it. But don't you see what you've done, Valarie? You've played right into their hands. They know that Candi didn't find that watch under a table. They figure you had the watch all along, and because things got hot, you decided to get somebody else to be the patsy and give it back to them."

"Harvey, you don't think—"

"I don't have to think! I know. You've just as much as signed your death certificate, Valarie. They're not going to let a cheap little junkie get by with trying to rip off their boss. They're convinced now that you're the one who ripped off that watch. It's been nice knowing you, Valarie!"

He let out a sinister laugh and headed back to his office.

I didn't know if he was trying to scare me or if he was serious. But I knew one thing. If they were coming back, I was not going to be there!

12

I went up to my room and grabbed my coat and purse. I started to pack, but I realized that would be a big mistake. Even if I wanted to leave to get away from those mob-type characters who were coming back, I knew that my biggest problem would be getting by Harvey and Angelo. Any kind of a suitcase would be a dead giveaway. And the word *dead* might not be too far wrong! If Harvey saw me, he'd shoot me in the back.

I wondered about Angelo. Was he my friend enough now that I could wrap him around my little finger? And what if I couldn't? What would it feel like to have someone break my legs—or my back? Would I end up paralyzed for life? Even the thought of it made me shudder with terror.

I carried my coat downstairs and sneaked through the hallway—so far so good. But when I got to the reception lounge, Candi was sitting there.

She spotted my coat and looked up questioningly.

"Just going to the drugstore," I said. "There's something I forgot to get. I'll be right back."

I put the coat on, thinking again how nice it would be to have a warm one! I hated going out and facing the bitter cold again, and it was sure going to be a lot worse in this threadbare rag I had to wear. I berated myself for not having the willpower to save up enough money to buy a warm coat as I had promised myself.

Willpower? What did a junkie know about that? Almost every penny I had made had gone for drugs. I knew I had about twenty-five dollars in my purse now. And it would probably go for drugs before the night was over.

Candi's laughter brought me back to the reality of the moment. "Yeah, you'll be right back," she said sarcastically, "in about ten minutes?"

"No, it'll probably be more like twenty minutes at the least," I replied, trying to sound casual about the matter so she wouldn't suspect anything.

"Who do you think you're kidding, Valarie?" she sneered. "It's been nice knowing you."

I leaned over her and whispered, "Candi, keep your big fat lip shut! You know Harvey's got every area around here bugged? You say something, and I'll bust your lip!"

"My lip has already been busted because of you!" she whispered back. "So don't you dare try anything else!"

She pointed to the swollen lip one of those goons had given her.

"You try anything, and I'm going to scream for Angelo!" she threatened. "The last time a girl tried to walk out of here, good old Angelo beat her up. I mean, he beat her to a pulp! He brought her back here, and then a few days later she just disappeared. I don't know if Angelo did her in, or if Harvey did it himself. But either way, she was gone—forever!" She let that last word sink in. "So don't start yelling about what you're going to do to me! Besides, you owe me some money. We made a deal, and. . . ."

That was the last thing I wanted to talk about, so I wheeled around and headed out the door. I didn't know if Candi would yell for Harvey and Angelo or not. It was a chance I just had to take.

The fierce wind that night added to my misery as it whipped through my coat, chilling me to the bone. I kept glancing over my shoulder, momentarily expecting Harvey or Angelo to appear. The farther I got from the Blue Lagoon, the better I felt. Every block decreased the chances of Harvey or Angelo finding me—at least for a while. Maybe if they did find me later and force me to go back, those two bodyguards of Harold Zolet's would have forgotten that caper with the watch.

I walked on down to Forty-second and Eighth. It was the only place I really knew. And I realized that if I spent the twenty-five dollars I had for dope, I was going to have to get some money for a place to stay—a place at least out of this biting wind. That meant going back to prostituting. What I had been doing hadn't been all that different, but back out here I no longer had protection by Angelo from the perverts. I'd have to locate a room somewhere. I'd have to stand out in the cold hustling. And I'd take a chance on the quality of the dope I could buy on the streets.

I leaned back against a building and surveyed my kingdom. It looked the same—dirty, depressing, degrading, and bone-chillingly cold.

Half a block away it seemed as though everybody was pushing dope. It didn't take me any time to make contact and buy a bag with my last twenty-five dollars.

Dumb me! How was I going to get off? I'd forgotten to bring my works! Now what was I going to do? I couldn't go back to the Blue Lagoon. Any pusher would charge me to rent a set of works. And I didn't have that kind of money.

Maybe if I watched to see where people went to get off, I could join them. Maybe they'd let me use their works.

About that time a guy and a girl bought and walked off. I tailed them into an alley where I saw them ducking into a doorway.

I waited a few minutes—so they would be in the middle of their fix. My plan just had to work. I could almost taste the dope. I wanted and needed that surge.

In a few minutes I headed toward where I had seen them disappear. Sure enough, there they were, both bent over on the cold, filthy ground. They looked like animals—no, they looked more like rats eagerly devouring food. If I hadn't been so anxious to get off myself, I would have been able to see what terrible problems dope causes for a person.

When I walked up, the guy had the needle in his arm. He saw me and jerked back, yelling, "Get out of here!"

I just smiled at him and said, "You're both under arrest!"

They jumped up and backed against the door.

The guy studied me for a moment and then snarled, "Look, you'd better have a backup. Because if you're not a cop, I'm going to kill you!"

Now my heart was beating so rapidly that I wondered if it might explode! Why had he made that threat? That wasn't a part of my plan. What's more, I'd made such an issue of the whole thing that I couldn't back down now.

"Don't get yourself into any worse trouble by making threats against a police officer," I warned. "Now, we're cleaning out this area of junkies. We've already busted ten tonight. My sergeant will be pleased with that. But it looks to me like young couples like you need a break. So if you two just take off, we should be able to forget the whole thing. You understand what I'm saying?"

The two nodded eagerly—saved from arrest by a non-cop!

The guy started to pick up his needle. Well, now, I couldn't have him do that.

"Look, you'd better leave the needle," I said confidentially. "It'd be real stupid of you to take it. I've got several cops outside the alley, waiting for me to flush the junkies out. If they search you and find that set of works, they'll throw the book at you. So just leave your works here and scram."

I pointed to the other end of the alley and told them, "Run like you've never run before! And don't you dare tell anybody I gave you two a break. Now get out of here this instant!"

They took off. I couldn't believe how gullible they were. All I said was that I was arresting them, and they took off like scared rabbits.

The needle they left behind still had junk in it. I jabbed it into my veins and got a hit right away. They had good stuff, and I'd got it! I'd have to remember this trick!

Back out on the street, I knew I had to hustle right away. I needed money for a room.

But when I stood on the corner, waiting for a trick, I happened to look down the street and saw the couple I had just ripped off heading my way! Hoping they hadn't spotted me yet, I turned away from them and started walking. If they saw me, they'd know I wasn't a cop. And I would be no match for the two of them. There was no telling what they might do to me. I'd forgotten what a jungle it was here on the streets.

Up ahead there was a subway entrance. Maybe if I ducked down there I could get rid of them. I didn't think they had spotted me yet, and they probably wouldn't be going into the subway.

I hurried down the steps, trying not to call too much attention to myself. But when I heard a train just pulling in, I thought, *Here's my way of escape!* I vaulted over the turnstile, and although the toll-booth operator yelled, I didn't even look back. I didn't have time to wait!

The train door was open, and I jumped right in and started walking. Looking back toward the turnstiles, I saw the couple I had ripped off. Apparently they had spotted me! Apparently they were following me because they were looking every which way. They weren't down here just to catch a train!

Finally the train door closed, and we took off. That couple was still out there. Relieved, I sat down. At least I was rid of them!

I got off on Houston Street. I knew there were a bunch of junkies around there. I guess it's true what they say—that misery loves company. I always kept looking for my kind.

But when I got up to the street from the subway, I realized I didn't know any of the people. And the place looked horrible. It certainly couldn't be any worse than Times Square, could it? I do know that I felt very ill at ease.

Noticing a bunch of girls standing around at a corner, I went up and joined them. This evidently was their contact point with the johns.

It worked a little different here. The guys would pull up in their cars, motion to a girl, and the girl would get into the car and take off with the guy. I didn't know where they were going, but I knew there must be money in it. And that's what I was interested in.

But none of the guys even looked at me. Maybe they had their regular girls. I sure wasn't having any luck.

Just when I was about to give up and try another location, a guy pulled up and motioned me to his car. When I got there, he rolled down the window and asked, "Want to go out?"

Now I was back to that old worry. Was he all right? I didn't know. But if I wanted to make any money, I would have to take that chance. So I opened the car door, slid in beside him, and we took off.

A couple of blocks away I said, "Got a place you want to go to?"

Without even looking at me, he replied, "Yeah, the docks."

The docks? Oh, no! I knew what happened down there! These guys would rape you and throw your body into the water. If there was one place I didn't want to go, it was to the docks. Suddenly that picture of Sheila overwhelmed me. That guy taking her down to the docks had been the last straw for her. I could still picture her lifeless body dangling from the bars of that jail cell. Poor Sheila. She said I'd be taking my life, too, sooner or later. Maybe she was right. What was there to live for?

Well, I sure didn't want any john making that decision for me. I didn't want to be beaten and raped and left for dead down on some deserted dock. If he didn't throw me into the river, I'd freeze in this bitter cold.

When he stopped at a light, I opened the door and leaped out, running down the street as fast as I could. I heard him start beeping his horn, but I didn't even look around.

I ran and I ran and I ran until I was completely out of breath. Exhausted, I leaned against a building and looked back. I couldn't see the guy anywhere, and I breathed a sigh of relief. I had escaped.

But my relief was short-lived. Because when I looked around, I saw burned-out tenements. Then I knew where I was—in the middle of the Lower East Side!

In this part of the city everybody looked dangerous, and probably was. The Lower East Side was a hellhole—junkies, muggers, rapists, murderers. I had to get out of here!

My mind was going like a whirlwind as I walked along that street. I was frightened of every shadow. I knew my life wasn't worth anything down here. I thought about my escape from the john who wanted to take me down to the docks and do who knew what. I thought about that couple I had escaped from. Then Harvey would still be looking for me. He'd kill me for walking out. Or he'd turn me over to Angelo, and he'd tear me limb from limb. Or those goons from the mob would find me and kill me because they thought I had ripped off their boss's watch.

I couldn't take a step without someone wanting to kill me! And as I walked along, I became aware that my life didn't mean very much to anybody else.

What chance did I have? If all those people who were after me didn't get me, then some john would finish me off somewhere. Or I'd get a hot shot and die. Or I'd end up like Sheila, dangling from my own blouse and jeans in a cell of some jail. Somehow I knew I didn't have very much longer to live!

Shivering in the cold, terrified for my life, and realizing I really didn't have any reason to live, I pulled my thin coat closer around me, and stuck my head in front of me to force my way into the wind. Talk about hitting bottom, I was there that night!

But as I walked, I heard something I hadn't heard in a long time—singing. People were singing—singing happy, joyful songs. What could anybody find to be happy about on a night like this?

The music was coming from a little storefront just ahead. Almost instinctively I hurried in its direction. And when I got there, I peered through the window. The people were clapping and singing and smiling. What was the matter with them? Didn't they know life was a dirty joke and there was nothing to be happy about?

I was about to walk on when the door opened and a young lady asked pleasantly, "Why don't you come in and join us?"

"Oh, no thank you, ma'am," I answered. "I just stopped to admire your music. It sounded real good on this cold night. And the people looked so happy."

"We're having a church service," she explained, "and it's open to anyone who wants to come."

"Oh, I thought maybe that's what it was," I said. "But I'm just not the type. You see, I don't go to church or anything like that. You know, I just wouldn't fit into a church."

She smiled and said, again so pleasantly, "Please don't feel that way. Everybody is welcome here. In fact, we're down here trying to help people who don't go to church."

I wondered what she meant by that. Happy people shouldn't be here on the Lower East Side—not in this hellhole!

I kept backing away, remembering the religious nuts who had approached me in the past when I'd been working the streets. I had often wondered if there was anything to what they claimed to have, but I'd never gotten into a serious conversation with any of them. I was always on the lookout for another trick and couldn't be bothered.

"It's awfully cold out here," she said. "Why don't you just step inside the door? We can talk there, if you want; or you can just get warm a few minutes. Nobody will make you stay against your will."

That was different. I'd just escaped from a place where I was a virtual slave—the Blue Lagoon.

I was cold, so I accepted her invitation, although somewhat reluctantly.

I was just beginning to relax a little, absorbing the welcome warmth, when she hit me with: "How long have you been on junk?"

That stunned me so that I just stammered around. I couldn't think of a reply.

"Excuse me for being so abrupt," she said, noticing my

discomfort. "But I used to have a terrible habit myself. I was a junkie for ten years."

I stared at her unbelievingly. She used to be a junkie? She looked so clean, so nice, so healthy. How was this possible?

"That's mighty nice for you," I said lamely. "I never did care much for junkies though. I mean, they're filthy people."

She smiled again as she said, "My name is Patti Vincent. I've been assigned to this mission by my school. I was saved five years ago, and I'll tell you, life's sure been different since then!"

I still couldn't believe what she was saying. There had to be a hitch somewhere. Things like that just didn't happen to junkies.

I figured maybe I'd better get away right now. Maybe this was a bunch of fanatics or something. Yet there was something so compelling about this Patti. I just couldn't figure her out.

She took my hand gently and asked, "What's your name?"

Why would she ask me that? Was she part of a plot to get me too? I almost lied, but then I realized no one had forced me to come to this place. If I thought she was part of a plot, I was the one getting paranoid!

"I'm Valarie Lambert," I said.

"Valarie! I'm so happy to meet you, Valarie. Now would you like to go over and sit down? I'll sit with you."

I started edging back toward the door, and she casually took my arm. "I know what you're thinking," she said. "You are thinking I'm a religious nut and you've got to watch out."

"Oh, no! Nothing like that!" I lied. "I mean, this religious bit is just not for me."

Patti laughed. "You sound just like I did five years ago, Valarie," she told me. "You see, that's what I thought when I was a junkie walking the streets, searching for answers. I had a ten-bag-a-day habit, Valarie. I know what it is to stand on the street and hustle. I've been beaten up by perverts. I used to work for a pimp who thought his thing was to beat me up all the time. I've done time. You name it, and I've been there. You may not believe this, Valarie, but I came to the end of myself when I was sitting in a jail cell, thinking about what a mess I'd made out of my life. I figured no one cared if I lived or died, so I started planning to take my own life."

Her story sounded so much like mine that I just couldn't believe it. But how could she know me that well?

"Then, Valarie, while I was sitting in that cell," she went on, "God performed a miracle for me. He sent a woman from the Walter Hoving Home to me."

Somewhere I'd heard that name.

Noticing my puzzled look, she explained, "The Walter Hoving Home is a home for girls upstate in Garrison. They take in girls who are addicts, prostitutes, alcoholics, delinquents—girls with problems—and try to help them see the difference Jesus can make in their lives. The wife of the director, Mrs. Benton, was the one who found me in jail. At first I didn't believe what she was trying to tell me either. But there was something about that woman that I just couldn't shake. She seemed to have answers that I didn't have.

"Would you believe she even came into my cell to talk to me? She seemed to understand what was going on in my head. And she made it so clear that Jesus was able to help me make something out of my life, that He would give me a purpose for living, that He would forgive my sins and make me all new. I couldn't believe it was true. But she prayed

with me there in that cell, and I received Jesus as my Saviour. Something happened within me right then and there.
I knew my sins were forgiven. And God took away my
habit—just like that!" She snapped her fingers. "Now you
know that's got to be a miracle. Right?"

I nodded before I realized what I was doing. But I knew
there was no point in protesting that I wasn't a junkie. This
girl had been around. She recognized me for what I was.

"And God performed other miracles for me," she went
on. "For instance, in court I was released to the custody of
the Walter Hoving Home. I spent a year there, going
through their program. That woman who led me to the
Lord—Mrs. Benton—I discovered that all the girls up there
call her Mom B. And she was just like a mother to me.

"Well, when I graduated from the Walter Hoving Home,
I went to Southeastern College in Lakeland, Florida. I got
my degree there, and now I'm back here, assigned to work
in this mission for a year to help girls like you."

"Like me?" I asked weakly.

"Yes, Valarie, like you. And I want you to know I've already sent five girls to the Walter Hoving Home. They've
realized, too, that Jesus can forgive their sins and make
them into something worthwhile."

Then she looked me straight in the eye and said quietly,
"Valarie, I believe God sent you here to me on purpose tonight. I believe you are going to be number six!"

If I live to be a hundred, I'll find it hard to believe I ever
said what I said next. I said, "Okay, I'm number six."

Smiling triumphantly, Patti took me by the arm and led
me to a nearby pew. I sat and listened as the singing continued. I tell you, it was absolutely glorious. I don't think
I'd ever heard singing like that before. I kept looking
around, studying the many happy faces. Some of the peo-

ple were almost glowing, they were so happy. I saw some with their eyes closed, their hands raised to heaven, and tears streaming down their cheeks. But I knew those were tears of joy, not of sorrow.

I eased out of my coat, half-thinking how nice it was to be in a warm place, out of the cold. And there was something contagious about being among happy people.

Then the minister spoke. I tried to follow what he said. I don't remember exactly all he said, but he made me realize that without God's help I'd never make anything out of my life. I knew that was right. I'd tried to do things my way all along, and it sure hadn't gotten me anywhere except into terrible messes.

At the close of his sermon he asked for those who were tired of their way of life to come forward to the altar and give their lives to Jesus. I knew that was what I wanted, so I moved out into the aisle and started forward. Patti was right beside me.

At the altar I knelt. Patti, kneeling beside me, explained how simple it was to be saved. The first thing I had to do, she said, was to admit I was a sinner. I certainly didn't have any problem with that. I knew I was a terrible sinner.

Then she explained I should ask Jesus to forgive me of my sins. I didn't have to name them one by one—just in a general way ask Him to forgive them all, and mean it.

Patti went on to tell me the third thing was to receive Jesus into my heart just by faith. She explained that He was knocking at my heart's door. If I would just open the door and invite Him in, He would come in. So I did it, believing that He really would do what I asked Him. And He came in. He really did. I knew it.

When I got up from that altar bench, I felt as if the weight of the whole world had been lifted from my shoulders. I felt so clean, so brand new, so full of life and hope.

Before I even had time to think about where I was going to spend the night, Patti said, "Valarie, you're coming to my apartment tonight. Then tomorrow we'll see about your being my number six to go to the Walter Hoving Home. Okay?"

I nodded, delighted for a place to spend the night, and looking forward to the future with hope—for the first time I could ever remember.

I was so excited I kept Patti up half the night, asking her questions about what being a Christian really meant. And I wanted to find out more about this Home where I might be going. She told me about their one-year program for girls like me. "They stress really learning to live according to the Bible," she told me. "You'll learn about the Christian life and how to live to please the Lord. It's such a loving, caring place."

I was the one plying Patti with questions, and she finally apologized for keeping *me* up so late!

I had noticed that she had just one single bed in her apartment. I'd figured I'd be sleeping on the couch or even the floor. But would you believe that she insisted I sleep in the bed? I protested, but she wouldn't hear of anything else. I began to see in Patti what a real Christian was like.

The next day she called the Walter Hoving Home and then drove me the ninety miles there. Of course, we talked all the way. When we were almost there, it hit me that I hadn't had any drugs since last night, and, furthermore, I wasn't craving any either! God had performed another miracle for me!

Patti told me it didn't always happen that way. Sometimes the girls went through kicking cold turkey. But the Lord helped them, too.

When we drove onto the grounds of the Walter Hoving Home, I thought I must be in heaven. I learned they have thirty-seven acres, lots of trees, a beautiful mansion, a swimming pool, horses to ride.

But my biggest surprise came when we walked in the door of the mansion. There stood a woman I immediately recognized. "Hey, I met you on the street a little while back," I said. "Aren't you the one they call Mom B?"

You should have seen her reaction. That huge smile broke across her face like the sunrise, and she came running toward me with open arms as she said, "And you're Valarie! I've never forgotten you, and I've been praying for you ever since that night we met on the street."

"I had no idea Patti was bringing me to the place you and that other girl—let's see, what was her name?"

"I believe Jennifer was with me that night."

"That's right! Jennifer! She used to work in a massage parlor, and she told me how the Lord had saved her. I never forgot that. Several times I wanted to contact you, but I had lost the brochure you gave me. I couldn't remember the name of the place. And to think that now I'm here with you!"

Tears brightened Mom B's eyes as she looked into mine and said, "Valarie, the Lord we serve is so good to us."

We were hugging each other, and both of us were crying now. Oh, it felt so good. I knew I'd come to a home of love—a real home that was going to help me grow and mature into the kind of a person God wanted me to be.

I guess all the girls who come to the Walter Hoving Home are special to Mom B and Brother B, but I felt as though I had a little extra love from them. Mom B was always hugging me. And Brother B always had a special greeting for me when we chatted about how I was getting

along. He'd say something like, "Hang in there!" or his
other specialty, "Have you got the victory?"

I learned to know the loving, caring staff at the home.
And I met a lot of other girls who, like me, had found that
Jesus Christ was able to change their lives completely.

My year at the home was a time of great adjustment. I
began learning a lot about myself, including the reasons I
had done some of the things I had done. But it was a year
of tremendous progress and growth in learning how to live
according to God's Word. I had never dreamed that the
Bible was so totally up-to-date, but I sure found that it had
all the help I needed for living.

I got another bonus at the home. Because they had a
state-accredited program there, I was able to finish my
high-school studies and be awarded my high-school di-
ploma at the same time that I finished the program there.

I had to make a court appearance during the time I was
at the home. But God worked another miracle. The judge
who heard my case was acquainted with the Bentons and
the work of the Walter Hoving Home. In fact, he had pre-
viously allowed some of the girls who came before him to
come to the home. So when he learned I was doing well at
the home, after I pleaded guilty to the charge of soliciting,
he suspended my sentence, on condition that I stay in the
program at the home and that he be sent regular reports of
my progress.

When I graduated from the Walter Hoving Home, I en-
rolled in Evangel College in Springfield, Missouri. It's a
Christian liberal-arts college, and I'm gaining more help in
living the Christian life, as well as getting a quality educa-
tion under the tutelage of Spirit-anointed teachers.

When I get my degree, I plan to go back to New York
City, the Lord willing. I'm going to be looking for Candi

and Martha and Cindy and girls like them. I want them to discover what I've found—that their lives can be changed dramatically for the good by the power of God.

I even hope to find old Harvey and talk to him about the Lord. Once when I was back in New York City, I drove by the old Blue Lagoon Massage Parlor and discovered it was boarded up. Maybe Harvey's expenses got to be more than his income. Maybe he ran into trouble with the mob. Maybe I'll never know if he's alive or dead. But when I get back to work in New York City, I'm going to be walking the streets and checking out the massage parlors. My guess is that Harvey's still operating one somewhere—probably under a different name. And maybe I'll run into Martha and Candi and Cindy—maybe even Angelo. After all, I've got some mighty important news to tell them. And when they see the change in me, I think they'll be willing to listen.

That important news is the reason I've been telling my story to you. I'm certainly not proud of the way I lived. I wouldn't even be telling it except that I want you to see that Jesus Christ can really make a difference in a person's life. I'm concerned about you, and I want you to know that Jesus can do for you what He's done for me.

Do you think it was just by chance you happened to pick up this book and read it? It's no more by chance than that meeting I had on the street with Mom B and Jennifer. It's no more by chance than Patti's inviting me into that church service. The circumstances of our lives are ordered by the Lord, and I believe that He saw the deep need in your life and brought about the circumstances that caused you to be reading about what happened to me.

Yes, I do believe that God had a hand in your reading about what happened to me. You see, what Jesus has done for me, He also wants to do for you. Maybe you're a junkie like I was. Maybe you've had enough sense not to get involved with the drug scene. I certainly hope so.

But junkies or not, in a way all of us are exactly the same. We're all sinners. And we all need to find salvation the same way, through the cross of Jesus Christ.

You see, Christ died on the cross for my sins and yours. He never sinned, but He died that we might have all our sins forgiven and be set free to really live. And let me tell you, I've never been more free in all my life than I've been since I've known Jesus as my Saviour. And I know He wants to make you free, too.

It's not hard to be free from your sin. Yet I remember how, as I stood listening to Patti that night, I almost blew it. I almost lost everything! Who knows what would have happened to me if I had turned away from God. I really believe I would have been dead before long.

But I'm alive today. And I'm really living. I've got a purpose, a reason, a hope. And you can have all that, too.

Here's all you have to do. First, admit you're a sinner. You know you are. Deep down inside you know you've said and done things that displease God. So admit to Him you're a sinner.

Then ask Jesus to forgive your sins. You don't have to name them all. Just pray, "Jesus, I'm a sinner, and I'm sorry that I've sinned. I ask You to forgive all my sins."

Then do what I did. By faith invite Jesus into your heart. Tell Him you want Him to take control of your life. And when you invite Him in, by faith believe that He really does come in to be your Lord and Saviour. That's what He's promised to do.

I felt free and forgiven and clean after I did that. I've talked to other Christians and learned that not everybody feels that way right at first. In fact, some girls told me they didn't feel one bit different at first. But that doesn't change the facts. It's as they taught us at the home: We live by faith, not by feelings. The faith has to come first; after that the feelings. Remember that. You are saved because you have come the way God has said in the Bible, not because of how you do or don't feel. That's where the faith comes in. It's taking God at His Word.

So if you've followed those three steps and sincerely meant each of them from your heart, whether you feel any different or not, something has happened. You've been saved, or as some people call it, born from above.

After you've made that commitment, find a good church to go to—a church where they believe and teach the Bible. And you should study the Bible at home, too. It will teach you how to live to please God.

There's something else. You also need to tell other people what the Lord has done for you. We learned at the home that this is called witnessing or testifying. I like to call it sharing the good news about Jesus.

Who knows? Maybe if you're out sharing the good news, I'll meet you out there. And we won't meet as junkies bound by the old debilitating habits. We'll meet as Christians redeemed by Jesus' death for us on the cross. Then together we can share the wonderful news of hope and life with those who feel that life has lost its purpose and meaning.

Realistically, of course, I know that the chances of our meeting are quite slim—at least on this earth. So we probably won't be working together. But I firmly believe that all Christians ought to be busy, involved, working to bring the lost sheep to the Good Shepherd.

The good news I possess—and that I hope you now also

possess—is something that we must share with those who are as hopeless as we once were.

Why do I feel so strongly about this? Look at it this way. I wouldn't be here today if people like Mom B, Jennifer, and Patti hadn't been concerned enough to share the Gospel with me!

The Walter Hoving Home.

Some good things are happening at The Walter Hoving Home.

Dramatic and beautiful changes have been taking place in the lives of many girls since the Home began in 1967. Ninety-four percent of the graduates who have come with problems such as narcotic addiction, alcoholism and delinquency have found release and happiness in a new way of living—with Christ. The continued success of this work is made possible through contributions from individuals who are concerned about helping a girl gain freedom from enslaving habits. Will you join with us in this work by sending a check?

The Walter Hoving Home
Box 194
Garrison, New York 10524
(914) 424-3674

Your Gifts Are Tax Deductible

Learn the Bible, challenge your wits, and have fun at the same time!